KIN

The Fantasy Tabletop Role-playing Game
Created by Veo Corva

First published in 2021 by Witch Key Fiction

ISBN: 978-1-9161009-9-2

Veo Corva

Website: https://veocorva.xyz

Witch Key Fiction

Website: https://witchkeyfiction.xyz

Cover art and section illustrations by Tithi Luadthong / Shutterstock.com

Character busts and sealorns by Eli Brown (Grim) (https://twitter.com/renardroi)

(Lizard person) Some artwork © 2020 Vagelio Kaliva, used with permission. All rights reserved.

White and gold dragon art by Heather Crook

Mage and cat image by MSzB / Shutterstock.com

Decorative black-and-gold line art by Kseniya Parkhimchyk / Shutterstock.com

Town and city maps created in Medieval Fantasy City Generator

World and continent maps made in Other World Mapper

Many thanks to the supporters of the

Non-Player Character Kickstarter campaign.

For information on creating game materials and stories within the world of *Kin*, check out the *Kin* Third Party License at https://veocorva.xyz

CONTENTS

೫ INTRODUCTION

ജ INTRODUCTION

The Associate Plane is a hub of magical activity, a contradiction of different sciences, different magics, different natures. It all comes together here. And the people of the Associate Plane understand better than anyone that what is strange is not necessarily threatening, and that what is beautiful can also be dangerous.

Welcome to the *Kin: The Fantasy Tabletop Role-playing Game. Kin* represents the web of universes of the Fractal Planes: inter-connected worlds with differing laws, magics, and inhabitants. Most games of *Kin* will concern Vanthis, a world in the Associate Plane, so known due to the large number of other planes it is not only adjacent to, but which it is so intertwined with that its inhabitants bear traits from those other worlds.

You, as the player, will navigate this world through Spells, Moves, and Plays, the tools of your trade. You will level up in order to learn new skills and proficiencies, whether they be magical or mortal in nature.

You, as the Game Master, will bring this world to life, describing scenes, voicing characters, and resolving the outcomes of player actions.

Kin is a universe waiting for a story. And you are the ones who will tell it.

> **Message from the author:**
>
> I wrote *Kin* to accompany my portal fantasy novel, *Non-Player Character,* since I had to work out the basic mechanics for the novel anyway. Whether you read *Non-Player Character* or not, I hope you'll enjoy this game.
>
> It absolutely spiralled out of my control into a fully-fledged TTRPG (well, maybe with a few awkward pinfeathers here and there). I'm delighted you're giving it a go.
>
> **With thanks and awkwardness,**
>
> **V**

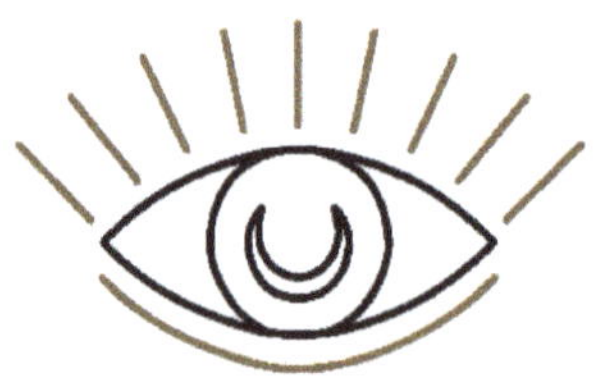

೫ HOW TO PLAY

✇ HOW TO PLAY

OBJECTIVE

The goal of the game is not to win, but to tell a compelling story which everyone involved enjoys. Sometimes that will mean quests go uncompleted, or goals will change. Sometimes Skill Checks will fail. A good story has high points and low points, and players are encouraged to embrace the drama of both.

As a player, you will be controlling one character and deciding what they do and what effect they have on the story. You will be doing your best to make decisions based on what the character knows and is motivated by, rather than by any outside knowledge you possess. Your ultimate goal within the game will depend on the character you have created.

As the Game Master, you will be controlling the world and all non-player characters within it. Your role is not to create the story so much as to create a framework for it, thereby co-creating the story with the players and responding to their actions. You want to set something up that has interesting (but ultimately surmountable) challenges for your players and which will have emotional resonance.

MECHANICS

Narrative Mode

This is unstructured storytelling which will make up the majority of gameplay. The Game Master will describe the environment and what is happening in it, and the players will describe what they do in response. When a player wants to do something which does not require an in-game mechanic to resolve, the Game Master will describe the outcome and how the player's actions affected the world. If the action involves other players, they will be able to respond in kind.

When a player wants to do something which does require an in-game mechanic to resolve (eg when a skill or proficiency is used) then the Game Master will ask the player to do so and will describe the outcome based on the result of that mechanic, usually on a sliding scale from critical failure to critical success.

See Example Play and Narrative Mode for more.

Action Mode

This is a structured action resolution mode which is used in moments where timing is critical, such as combat, chase-sequences, or time-sensitive puzzles. It is defined by 'rounds', during which players must take and respond to actions. The Game Master will signal the switch to Action Mode by asking the players to 'queue'.

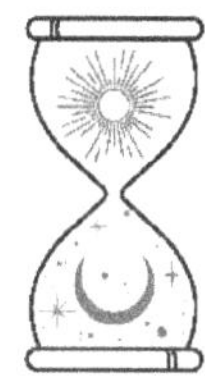

Queuing

Queuing is when players must decide between themselves in what order they will take their turn. This should be a snap judgement rather than discussion, and a note should be made of the order. Any other actors in this mode (such as NPCs controlled by the Game Master) should be added to the queue depending on both the narrative context and how efficiently the players queue.

Turn-based rounds

While in this mode, each player will get 1 turn per round, during which they will be able to take actions limited by their skills, proficiencies, and how many Action Points and Energy Points they have to spend. At the end of the round, Action Points refresh.

Smooth Action Mode and Strategic Action Mode

There are two options for Action Mode: Smooth and Strategic. Smooth Mode resolves faster and is less focused on mechanics. Strategic Mode takes longer and relies heavily on mechanics. Both have different strengths, and potentially different uses. The Game Master will specify which mode is being used when asking players to queue for combat.

See Action Mode for more detail.

Dice-Rolling: Skill Checks

Outcomes in *Kin* are determined by dice-rolling. Every time a player wants to attempt something challenging, the Game Master must determine which skill it falls under, and the player must make a roll. The difficulty of each of these Skill Checks is determined either by the game or by the Game Master.

Your skills in *Kin* are as follows:

Body Skills: Agility, Thievery, Stealth, Endurance, Threaten

Mind Skills: Convince, Alchemy, Search, Scholar, Nature

Soul Skills: Liar, Wild Empathy, Social Instinct, Perform, Create

There are two main dice you roll in the course of making a Skill Check.

Checks and Rolls: Quick Reference

Skill Checks	Rolled to determine the outcome of a skill. Some proficiencies may modify the result.	Skill die + Fate die = Skill Check total.
Stat Checks	Rolled when there is not an applicable skill or when called for by a proficiency.	Stat + Fate die = Stat Check total.
Attack Check	Rolled when making an attack. Must be higher than the target's Defence to succeed. Some proficiencies may modify the result.	Weapon Die* + Fate Die = Attack Check total. *When there is no weapon die, add +0 (no weapon) or +1 (when using a weapon) instead.
Fate 20 / Critical Success	When a Fate Die lands on 20, the check becomes a Critical Success. For an attack check, this automatically hits and deals an additional Wound.	
Fate 1 / Critical Failure	When a Fate Die lands on 1, the check becomes a Critical Failure. For an attack check, this automatically misses.	

The Dice

Skill dice represent your skill and are determined by the number of points you have invested into a given skill. If you have invested 0 points in the skill, then you do not roll a skill die. If you have invested 1 point, you use the Novice die (d4), 2 points you use the

Apprentice die (d6), etc. Please see the below table which determines which die is used at which skill level.

Under normal circumstances, only 1 skill die will be rolled as part of a Skill Check. However some situations will mean you have **Favour.** In the case of Favour, you may roll your skill die twice and take the higher of the two values.

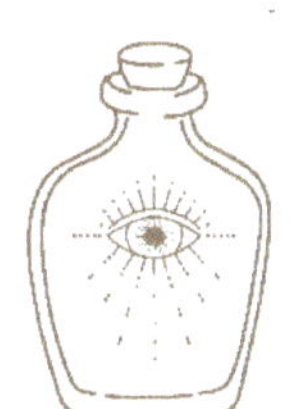

Fate dice represent chance and are always rolled when making a Skill Check. Under normal circumstances, only 1 fate die will be rolled as part of a Skill Check. However, some situations will mean that you have **Luck.** In the case that you spend a Luck point, you may roll your fate die twice and take the higher of the two values. You may decide to do this after you have rolled a Skill Check, but it must be before the result has been determined by the Game Master.

Skill Dice		
Die	Skill Points	Skill Level
d4	1	Novice
d6	2	Apprentice
d8	3	Adept
d10	4	Expert
d12	5	Master
d20	-	- (Fate die, rolled with every check)

Critical Rolls

Your fate die has the chance of making a roll **critical.** If your fate die rolls a 20, you have critically succeeded. If your fate die rolls a 1, you have critically failed.

Critical Fate Rolls (d20)	
Roll	Result
20	Critical Success
1	Critical Failure

A **Fate 20** is an automatic success, and a **Fate 1** is an automatic failure. However, this doesn't necessarily mean what it seems at face value.

A critical success at something impossible or incredibly foolish (think jumping off a cliff and flapping your arms to fly) might just mean you don't fail as spectacularly as you would have (for example, your flailing arm snags on a root, preventing you from falling to your death).

A critical failure at something very simple (think, jumping over a small gap) might mean that you still succeed, but inelegantly or with embarrassment (think, you stub your toe and fall over to the other side).

It's up to the Game Master to determine the outcome of all rolls, but they should take special care to understand that critical rolls do not break the laws of the game or suspension of disbelief. Though, of course, faking out players with an initial joke answer in especially ridiculous scenarios is encouraged.

Outcome

The combined result of your **skill** and **fate** rolls represents your Skill Check, and its success or failure will depend on the difficulty of the check and whether you had a critical success or a critical failure. Some proficiencies or circumstances (such as Favour or Luck) will also contribute to the final outcome. As a rule, if you meet or exceed the Skill Check Difficulty, you have succeeded. Higher margins of success lead to more impressive success, with Critical Success being the best possible result.

In general, higher rolls are better. The Game Master may choose to allow failed checks to succeed or successful checks to fail, depending on their circumstances.

It is up to the Game Master to **describe** the outcome. Not just whether you succeeded, but what success looks like. This can include flair (particularly when there is a critical roll involved) but should not misconstrue the original intention of the player.

The players should not know the difficulty of the check before they roll and do not need to know the difficulty after. All they need to know is the outcome.

Skill Check Difficulty		
Total Roll Required	Difficulty	Example
10	Simple	A Search check to look for treasure in a large but well-lit room.
15	Intermediate	A Social Instinct check to tell whether the person who has hired you is telling the truth.
20	Challenging	A Thievery check to steal a key from a guard.
25	Masterful	A Wild Empathy check to calm and ride a wild wyvern.
26+	Legendary	An Endurance check to catch a falling boulder that would have crushed you.
*This is a rough guide. Actual difficulties may fall between these numbers depending on what Game Master specifically has in mind. **Not all actions will require a Skill Check. A Game Master should only ask for a Skill Check when there is an element of challenge or a chance of failure.		

Luck and Favour

Luck and Favour both represent moments where you make additional dice rolls in the hopes of getting a more favourable result.

Favour refers to your skill die. If you roll with favour, you roll your skill die twice, taking the higher value. Favour is given by the Game Master in situations where the player making the check has particular expertise or is receiving assistance from another player. Unlike Luck, Favour cannot be saved. It applies to a particular roll, and then is gone.

Game Masters are encouraged to give Favour when it seems that the player should be more likely to succeed on a particular roll.

 **Luck** refers to your Fate die. Luck is given not at the time that a roll is made, but as a resource to be saved. Luck is tracked on the character sheet, and resets to 0 at the end of each full rest. When you make a Skill Check, you may spend a Luck point to re-roll the Fate die and take the higher value. You may only use 1 Luck per Skill Check. Luck may be spent after a Skill Check has been rolled, but it must be used before the Game Master has determined the result of that check.

Game Masters are encouraged to give Luck whenever a player shows particular moral integrity, undergoes personal growth, or has dealt with something in a clever manner. It is the main reward mechanic of the game. Game Masters may also take away Luck where deemed appropriate, though a player's Luck can never go below zero.

Stat Checks

Some proficiencies or situations may call for a Stat Check. A Stat Check is more broad than a Skill Check, and does not use additional dice.

When making a Stat Check against a Difficulty, players roll a Fate die and add the relevant Stat (Body for a Body Check, Soul for a Soul Check, etc).

Stat Checks		
Opposed Stat Checks	Used when called for by a Proficiency.	Target must roll Stat + Fate die versus the user's Stat + 10. If the target's total meets or exceeds the user's, the ability is resisted. EP is still consumed.
General Stat Checks	Used when a check is required but there is no appropriate skill	Player rolls Stat + Fate die versus a difficulty, as with a skill. Of note: Stats are more reliably high than Skills, so a GM may choose to raise the difficulty accordingly (eg +5).

When making a Stat Check in opposition to a proficiency (eg a Mind Check versus a Charm Mind spell) you roll versus the caster's Mind + 10, and if your roll equals or exceeds the caster's, you succeed.

Stat Checks are largely restricted to certain proficiencies, but a Game Master may choose to use one at any time where they seem relevant.

<u>Attack Checks</u>

If you wish to attack someone, you may be required to make an Attack Check. Attack Checks are made by rolling Weapon Die + Fate 20. If it equals or exceeds the target's Defence, the attack hits and will deal a Wound (or more, if Critical).

If you do not have a Weapon Die due to not taking the Melee Specialist or Ranged Specialist proficiencies, then replace the Weapon Die with 0 when not using a weapon, or a 1 when using a weapon.

Proficiencies: Spells, Moves, & Plays

In addition to skills, proficiencies are the main way that players can interact with the world. They are purchased at character creation and when levelling up in a similar manner to skills (see Levelling Up below).

Proficiencies are divided into three main categories: Spells, Moves, and Plays. These categories are more aesthetic than anything, as any player may purchase a proficiency from any category, providing their character meets the necessary Stat Requirements for that proficiency and has the Proficiency Point to spend.

Proficiencies are a kind of special action. Unlike Skill Checks and basic attacks, they often require a player to spend Energy Points (EP) to use them. This means that the amount that they can be used in a day is limited. A Proficiency can be used at any time provided the player has that proficiency and has the required EP to use it.

Some proficiencies are magical, while some are unmagical. Each proficiency has a described effect and, in some instances, use-case.

See <u>Proficiencies: Choosing What Makes You Special</u> for more information.

LEVELLING UP

Character progression is marked mechanically through levelling up. Each new level unlocks new proficiencies, skills, and stats. New levels may also award more Action Points, enabling characters to use more powerful proficiencies and take more actions in Action Mode.

Levelling up should happen for all players at the same time, to maintain balance within the group and acknowledge and encourage support for each other's progression and personal storylines.

Players should only gain new levels when they complete significant emotional or challenging story arcs. Significant story arcs do not necessarily mean combat.

Indeed, completing a several-episode arc to reconcile with someone one of the players hurt in the past or seeking out long-lost family members is even more significant than defeating a powerful enemy in battle, and should be treated as such.

For players to be rewarded for defeating enemies in combat, it must contain an emotional component for their characters, and should ideally resolve an ongoing arc.

Level Progression is as follows:

Levelling Up				
Level	Stat Points	Proficiency Points	Total Action Points	Total Energy Points
1 (Character Creation)	5	2	1	6
2	+1	+1	1	7
3	+1	+1	1	8
4	+1	+1	1	9
5	+2	+1	2	10
6	+1	+1	2	11
7	+1	+1	2	12
8	+1	+1	2	13
9	+1	+1	2	14
10	+2	+2	3	15
11	+1	+1	3	16
12	+1	+1	3	17
13	+1	+1	3	18
14	+1	+1	3	19
15	+2	+1	4	20
16	+1	+1	4	21
17	+1	+1	4	22
18	+1	+1	4	23
19	+1	+1	4	24
20	+2	+2	5	25

EXAMPLE PLAY

See below a script showing a snippet from an example game of Kin. *The scenario here is that the players were hired to prevent a supposed 'haunting' from ruining Lady Eyamar's ball.*

Game Master Pauline: You are shown into the ballroom. Glittering chandeliers hang from the ceiling, each overgrown with beautiful fey flowers. Instead of pillars, trees stud the room, their canopies arching across the ceiling. The whole room feels bright and fresh. A few pairs of dancers twirl across the floor, but most are at the sidelines, talking in groups.

Hanna (playing Hanley): Woah.

Game Master Pauline: A feykin woman with the wings and features of a humanoid bat approaches. She wears a sparkling blue dress. It is Lady Eyamar. She snaps a fan open and fans herself, looking harried. 'Good, you've finally arrived! We need to get people dancing. They're being dreadfully boring. Pair up or find a partner, would you?'

Rex (playing Ram): I say: 'We're not here for that.'

Game Master Pauline: She looks shocked. 'Pardon?'

Kenta (playing Kendallien): Kendallien is *not* going to dance …

Game Master Pauline: Keep it in-character, please.

Kenta (playing Kendallien): I square my shoulders, showing how much larger than her I am. I say: 'Leave. We're working.'

Hanna (playing Hanley): 'Kendallien!'

Rex (playing Ram): Excellent.

Game Master Pauline: Kendallien, make a Threaten check for me.

Kenta (playing Kendallien): I rolled a 5 on Fate, plus a 4 on my skill die. So 9 total.

Rex (playing Ram): Use Luck!

Kenta (playing Kendallien): I'm out of Luck.

Game Master Pauline: Lady Eyamar continues to fan herself, giving you a look full of lazy disgust, as if she can hardly be bothered to acknowledge you. 'Perhaps you would prefer to leave?' she says. 'And I'll handle this so-called "ghost" myself.'

Kenta (playing Kendallien): I stare at my feet and mumble in response. That look slayed me.

Hanna (playing Hanley): 'Lady Eyamar, please forgive my companions. They are loutish and taciturn but I'm sure would make adequate dancers. After all,' and I glare at them now, 'it would make it easier to move around the hall without attracting undue attention. They'll dance with each other, of course.'

Kenta (playing Kendallien): I am still too unnerved by Lady Eyamar to protest.

Rex (playing Ram): I just say: '... Fine.'

Hanna (playing Hanley): 'And of course, Lady Eyamar, I will be dancing with *you*.' And I wink at her.

Game Master Pauline: Make a Convince check. With Favour, because she already liked you best.

Hanna (playing Hanley): Let's see … I use my Flirtatious proficiency as well for +3, since I winked … and I hate that Fate roll, I spend a Luck to roll again … that's 21 total!

Game Master Pauline: 21 … all right. To your surprise, Lady Eyamar, who has always been so reserved, actually blushes. She holds out her hand. 'I think you might dance very adequately indeed,' she says.

Kenta (playing Kendallien): Oooh!

Rex (playing Ram): No! She's the worst!

Hanna (playing Hanley): She's paying us!

Game Master Pauline: Keep it in character please. Okay so you all go out on the dance floor? Good. I'll make this a Smooth Action Mode scene. Queue up and let me know what you're doing to either look for signs of the haunting or blend in at the ball and I'll tell you how the next hour works out …

Rex (playing Ram): Well I'll go first.

Hanna (playing Hanley): Then me!

Kenta (playing Kendallien): Guess I'll go last.

Game Master Pauline: Okay. Ram, what do you do?

Rex (playing Ram): As soon as Lady Eyamar is distracted by Hanley, I break away from Kendallien and sneak into the rest of the manor to look for the ghost. I cast Illusion to turn myself invisible.

Hanna (playing Hanley): What? No! She'll be furious if we sneak off!

Game Master Pauline: Too late, he's already done it. Ram, roll Search. Who's next?

End of example play.

SAFETY

It's important to ensure that the game is safe and comfortable for all involved. For this reason, the GM and players must have a conversation about what kind of game they want to play prior to starting – what they are comfortable roleplaying, and what they are not, how long each session should be, what they expect from the game, etc.

Further, it is important to have a safety system in place so that players can signal if they are uncomfortable with something that is happening or need to stop for another reason. For some groups, this might be private messaging or texting the GM. Sometimes this means putting an X in chat to signal discomfort, or raising your hand. The important thing is that there is a system in place that everyone is comfortable with, and that all players and the GM are clear on what to do.

HOUSE-RULING

Finally, a reminder of the importance of house-ruling. This guide will not have a rule for every situation. The rules here might not suit how you want to play. Perhaps there are additional rules you would like to include in your games; perhaps there are existing rules you would prefer to omit.

This is referred to as 'house-ruling'. It is entirely legal within the bounds of a *Kin* game. The rules exist to create the game; the game is supposed to be fun. If the game would be more fun with tweaked rules, then you should feel free to do so within your own games.

Ultimately, the Game Master has the deciding power over what the rules of their personal *Kin* games are, and may change, break, or bend them as they please. Always with the understanding that the game should be *fun* and above-all *safe* for all involved.

> **Tip: Consistency is key. Players will feel more confident of their ability to navigate the game world when the rules are not constantly changing. Bear that in mind when creating house-rules, and ensure all players are clear on what the rules are.**

ॐ CHARACTER CREATION

CHARACTER CREATION

Character Creation will help you build your character sheet and progress your character as you level up. It encompasses both the mechanical side of your character and the narrative side — think not just what you character can do, but who they are and what they want.

Levelling Up				
Level	Stat Points	Proficiency Points	Total Action Points	Total Energy Points
1	5	2	1	6
2	+1	+1	1	7
3	+1	+1	1	8
4	+1	+1	1	9
5	+2	+1	2	10
6	+1	+1	2	11
7	+1	+1	2	12
8	+1	+1	2	13
9	+1	+1	2	14
10	+2	+2	3	15
11	+1	+1	3	16
12	+1	+1	3	17
13	+1	+1	3	18
14	+1	+1	3	19
15	+2	+1	4	20
16	+1	+1	4	21
17	+1	+1	4	22
18	+1	+1	4	23
19	+1	+1	4	24
20	+2	+2	5	25

PLANARKIN: CHOOSING YOUR MAGICAL ORIGIN

Within the world of *Kin,* all living creatures are kin in some way to other planes. Sometimes this is literal, as when someone's grandmother was a faerie princess. Sometimes this is stranger, as when you were born near a portal to the Void Between Worlds and developed Void-like traits as a result. Sometimes this happens later in life: people become cursed or exposed to extraplanar magic.

There is little consistency about it. There are too many sources, and it's rare that someone is kin to only one plane. Indeed, even parents and children can show wildly different traits, so two feykin might have an astralkin child, though neither parent showed much in the way of astralkin traits.

Player characters in *Kin* are typically humans who have magically mutated into feykin, astralkin, or voidkin. Some people look closer to unaltered humans and have only minor physical traits, while others look almost like another species entirely. Again, this can vary even between blood relatives.

It is therefore best described as a kind of shorthand for certain collections of magical traits and appearances, and it is treated similarly to how one might describe hair or eye colour on Earth.

Feykin

Feykin are people who primarily exhibit features associated with the Fey Plane of The Glamouring. This includes elemental-like features, plant-like features, and animal-like features. A human who has the legs of a goat might be feykin, or one who looks like a bipedal wolf, but so also might someone who has vines instead of hair. A feykin might also be someone with long pointed ears, such as might traditionally be associated with an elf.

Traditionally feykin traits might include the ability to walk on water, wings, or the ability to speak to plants. Those with primarily feykin traits inherently speak Fey language.

Astralkin

Astralkin are people who primarily exhibit features associated with the Astral Plane of The Astralar. This includes sparkling skin, glowing eyes or general aura, energy-like features such as hair that appears to be made of night sky. There is some overlap with fey features, particularly in regard to aquatic features, as many beings of the Astralar have seemingly aquatic shapes. This can include scales, tails, or similar.

Traits traditionally associated with astralkin might include the ability to see in the dark, produce light, or control water. Those with primarily astralkin traits inherently speak Astral language.

Voidkin

Voidkin are people who primarily exhibit features associated with The Void Between Worlds, a plane or series of planes of which little is known beyond that it is vast, empty, and dark. This includes ghostly light, translucence, and shadows. There is some overlap with astralkin and feykin in the features of horns, scales, tentacles, and similar.

Traits traditionally associated with the Void might include a shadowy aura, the ability to teleport short distances, or to walk through walls. Those with primarily Voidkin traits inherently speak Voidspeech language.

Tip: For more information about the planes that influence the people of Vanthis, please see The World of Vanthis: The Planes.

TRAITS: CHOOSING YOUR INNATE MAGIC

Your traits are your innate magical abilities, things you didn't have to learn. Some may cost EP and AP to use, and some won't.

You should think about traits that fit well with your chosen origin, and that will make for interesting gameplay with your particular character. Interesting doesn't necessarily mean optimised — sometimes traits that have nothing to do with the skills and proficiencies you choose will make for the best story or character moments.

You have **3 Trait Points** to spend at character creation and you will not receive any more trait points after spending these. You may choose not to spend your trait points if you wish, but after character creation, those points are lost forever.

Tip: If you have a trait in mind that does not appear on this list, you may work with your Game Master to determine its mechanics and cost, bearing in mind that more powerful traits will cost 3 points, and less powerful will cost only 1 trait point. The Game Master makes the final call on which custom traits are allowed or disallowed, and on their mechanics and costs.

Trait List

Aquatic Native

You have an aquatic tail, webbed hands / feet, or other adaptation that makes swimming in water significantly faster. All movement in water takes 1 less AP per range (with a minimum of 0), and you are considered twice as fast while in water.

Trait Point Cost: 1

Bend Water

You can manipulate small amounts of water without touching it. You can move, freeze, or heat up to a litre of water as long as it is nearby and within sight. You cannot manipulate enough to cause a Wound.

Range: Nearby
AP per use: 1
Trait Point Cost: 1

Bend Fire

You can manipulate small amounts of fire without touching it. You can start, extinguish, colour-change and move up to a handful of flame as long as it is nearby and within sight. You cannot manipulate enough to cause a Wound.

Range: Nearby
AP per use: 1
Trait Point Cost: 1

Blink

You can teleport a Long distance in any direction without passing through the intervening spaces. This is limited by your line of sight.

Range: Long
EP per use: 3
AP per use: 1
Trait Point Cost: 2

Claws

You have claws strong enough to act as weapons and you gain +1 to Attack Checks with them.

Trait Point Cost: 1

Darksight

You have the ability to see in the dark. You lose some of your colour perception in darkness but none of your general acuity.

Trait Point Cost: 1

Dual Forms

You can shapeshift at will between two distinct forms, though both must be humanoid / anthropomorphic in nature. You gain two additional trait points which are available only in your second form.

AP per use: 1
Trait Point Cost: 2

Elemental Resistance

You are resistant to one form of elemental damage — fire, ice, earth, or air. Attacks of this type do 1 less Wound to you.

Trait Point Cost: 3

Fixed Invisibility

You have the ability to become invisible — but only for as long as you do not move. You can remain invisible for as long as you hold your breath and freeze in place.

EP per use: 3
Trait Point Cost: 2

Flight

You have flight-capable wings, the ability to fly without wings, swim through the air, or other means of travelling aerially. This is a natural form of movement for you and costs the same AP as would normal movement, and at the same speed.

EP per use: 1 (only costs EP when taking off / activating)
Trait Point Cost: 3

Ghostwalk

You can become ethereal and pass through solid objects for as long as you can hold your breath. Every non-living thing you carry on your person (eg clothing, pack) goes with you. You can only remain ethereal for as long as you can hold your breath. You cannot become physical again until your entire body is un-occluded, and you cannot see while your eyes are inside a solid object. You will be forcefully ejected into the nearest free space and back into your physical form when your breath runs out.

EP per use: 3
AP per use: 1
Trait Point Cost: 3

Levitation

You are able to hover as much as 2 feet above the ground at will. This also enables you to glide or fall more slowly. This could be due to wings or other sources.

Trait Point Cost: 1

Long Shadow

You are able to create or deepen shadows in your immediate vicinity. This could be an extension of a shadow aura, your natural shadow, or from another source. You can use this to obscure yourself. Your shadow does not affect your vision when used in this way but does affect others, who have a -2 to attacks against you while the effect is active.

Range: Close (on self)
EP per round: 1 (when used to obscure, 0 when not)
AP per use: 1
Trait Point Cost: 1

Natural Armour

Your skin, scales, bark or similar is unusually tough and difficult to pierce, providing you with natural armour. When a critical attack is rolled against you, roll a Fate die. If it is less than 10, the attack is no longer critical and will do normal damage.

Trait Point Cost: 2

Plant Speaker

You have the ability to speak to plants, and the plants will understand you. You must make a successful Wild Empathy check any time you wish to convince a plant of something, and you cannot persuade a plant to do something it is physically incapable of (such as moving or growing faster, though this depends on the plant). The plant cannot verbally communicate back unless it is a plant naturally capable of speech.

Trait Point Cost: 1

Prehensile Appendage

You have a prehensile tail, tentacle, trunk or similar, which is able to act as an additional arm / hand for the purposes of taking actions, holding things, climbing, etc. You may take this trait multiple times at the same cost. You gain +1 to all Skill Checks where the additional appendage would be advantageous.

Trait Point Cost: 1

Shining Aura

You are able to create or brighten light in your immediate vicinity. This could be an extension of a bright aura around you or be from another source. You can use this to obscure yourself. Your aura does not affect your vision when used in this way but does affect others, who have a -2 to attacks against you while the effect is active.

Range: Close (on self)
EP per round: 1 (when used to obscure, 0 when not)
AP per use: 1
Trait Point Cost: 1

Siren Song

You have a captivating singing voice that attracts the attention of any creature that hears it. Listeners must make a Mind Check (Mind stat + Fate die) equal to your Soul stat + 10, or else they will be completely distracted. They may repeat this check every round. If the listener takes damage, the effect ends. You gain +5 on Perform checks that involve singing whenever you activate this trait.

Range: Nearby.
EP per round: 3
AP per round: 1
Trait Point Cost: 1

Speedy

You are unusually quick on land. This could be due to having more legs or another source. Movement costs 1 less AP per range with a minimum of 0. You can also Sprint for 5 EP which will move you a Far distance for only 1 AP.

EP per use: 3 (Sprint only)
Trait Point Cost: 3

Telekinesis

You can magically manipulate any object within sight and range that you would be able to freely lift with one hand. This includes manipulating parts of a larger object. You cannot manipulate it with enough force to cause a Wound.

Range: Nearby
EP per use: 1
AP per use: 1
Trait Point Cost: 1

Telepathy

You are able to speak directly into the mind of any creature within sight or whom you know to be Close. If they are capable of speech, they understand your words, regardless of language. If they wish to ignore you, they can make a Mind Check (Mind stat + Fate die) against your Mind stat + 10 and on a success, they no longer hear your telepathy for the next hour.

Range: within sight
EP per use: 1
AP per use: 0
Trait Point Cost: 3

Waterwalk

You are able to walk on water and liquids of a similar density at will. If you allow yourself to sink into water, you must breach the surface before you can re-activate this effect.

Trait Point Cost: 1

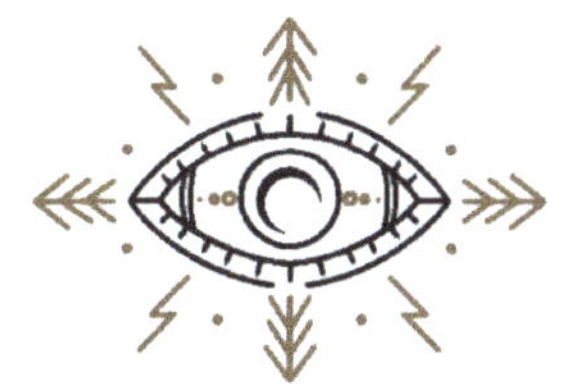

STATS: CHOOSING YOUR STRENGTHS

Within *Kin,* there are only 3 Stats: Body, Mind, and Soul. Think of these as the basic building blocks of your character. Each of these stats heads a category of skills and contributes toward minimum requirements for proficiencies.

At Character Creation, you get 5 Stat Points to distribute as you please among these Stats. For each point you put into a Stat, you gain a Skill Point to spend in the corresponding Skill Category (eg 1 point in Body stat = 1 point to spend in a Body skill). This rule of 1 Skill Point per Stat Point will continue throughout levelling.

Proficiencies are also restricted by Stat prerequisites, and many proficiencies have prerequisites from more than one Stat.

In gameplay, you will roll Stat checks to defend yourself from certain proficiencies. Body, Mind, and Soul all defend against different kinds of proficiencies, and all are valuable to your defence.

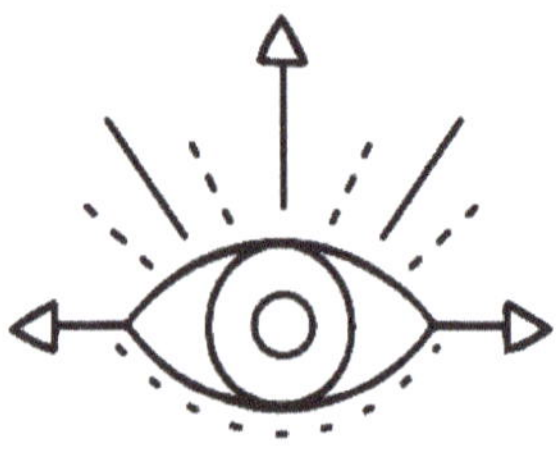

Body

Your Body stat represents your physicality. Whether you are quick or strong or endurant or dextrous, Body determines it all. Consequently, Body governs the most Move proficiencies.

As Body is a very broad category, it is up to you what it does and doesn't mean. If you desire your character to be quick and dextrous but do not want them to be strong, that is your call. If you want it to mean that you are all around amazing at physical things; well, that's up to you as well.

Body skills: Agility, Thievery, Stealth, Endurance, Threaten

Mind

Your Mind stat represents your mental prowess. Whether you are studious or strong-willed or wise, Mind determines it all. Consequently, Mind governs the most Spell proficiencies.

As Mind is a very broad category, it is up to you what it does and doesn't mean. If you desire your character to be thoughtful but do not want them to be scholarly, that is your call.

If you want it to mean that you are all around amazing at all things mental; well, that's up to you as well.

Soul

Your Soul stat represents your sense of self. Whether you are charismatic or creative or spiritual, Soul determines it all. Consequently, Soul governs the most Play proficiencies.

As Soul is a very broad category, it is up to you what it does and doesn't mean. If you desire your character to be artistic but do not want them to be personable, that is your call. If you want it to mean that you are all around amazing at all things soul; well, that's up to you as well.

SKILLS: CHOOSING WHAT YOU'RE PRACTICED AT

Skills are the main way you will interact with the world. They represent your knowledge, your training, and your experience. Accordingly, they will grow with time.

Every skill is governed by a corresponding stat: Body, Mind, or Soul. Every time you put a point in a stat, you also gain 1 Skill Point to spend in one of the skills it governs. So for example, if you put a stat point in Body, you can also put a Skill Point in either Agility, Thievery, Stealth, Endurance, or Threaten.

Skills are more specific than stats, but are still used in a broad array of scenarios and to fulfill a variety of in-game needs. Ultimately, it is up to your Game Master which skill is called for, and when, but a description of what each skill is broadly for is below.

Body Skills

Agility

Agility represents physical dexterity, acrobatics, and speed. You may be asked to roll an agility check when attempting to jump a chasm, or dodge a projectile, or out-run a pursuer. You may also be asked to roll an Agility check when juggling, or playing horseshoes, or catching a thrown item.

Thievery

Thievery represents your skill in criminal activities. You may be asked to roll a Thievery check when attempting to pick locks (or pockets), when attempting to steal something from a shop counter unnoticed, or when attempting to disable a trap. You may also be asked to roll Thievery when determining where is best to sell stolen items, when determining your knowledge of local criminal groups, or when attempting to acquire illegal items.

Stealth

Stealth represents your skill to hide and move quietly. You may be asked to roll a Stealth check when hiding under a bed, or when sneaking up on a sleeping guard. You may also be asked to roll Stealth when attempting to hide someone else under a pile of leaves, or when determining the best place to bury treasure.

Endurance

Endurance represents your strength, stamina, and tolerance. You may be asked to roll an Endurance check when trying to move a boulder blocking your path, or when running long-distance without breaks. You may also be asked to roll an Endurance check when tolerating unexpected pain, when carrying someone to safety, or when deciding how much alcohol you can handle.

Threaten

Threaten represents your ability to physically intimidate or frighten. You may be asked to roll Threaten when making yourself look big to frighten away wolves, or when convincing an attacker to back down, or when trying to shake someone down for money.

Mind Skills

Convince

Convince represents your persuasiveness and skill with spoken word. You may be asked to roll Convince when negotiating a peace treaty, or when explaining to a troll why you would taste terrible, or when convincing a group of bandits to take the money you offer and start a peaceful life.

Alchemy

Alchemy represents your skill with identifying the properties of chemicals and ingredients, and your ability to use the same to create potions, salves, and elixirs. You may be asked to roll Alchemy when creating a healing potion or when attempting to discern the effects of an unlabelled potion.

Search

Search represents your perceptiveness and ability to find things in an unknown environment. You may be asked to roll Search when looking for a specific item in a huge pile of junk, or when rifling through a study looking for evidence. You may also be asked to roll Search when keeping watch for enemies while travelling through the forest.

Scholar

Scholar represents your academic knowledge and ability to learn through reading. You may be asked to roll Scholar when trying to remember the history of a legendary sword, or when drawing on theoretical knowledge of magic. You may also be asked to roll Scholar when spending a day researching in the library, or when giving an academic presentation.

Nature

Nature represents your knowledge of and ability to survive in natural environments. You may be asked to roll Nature when determining whether a flower is deadly poison or delicious tea, or when identifying the species of the strange seal-like creature that visits you in the night. You may also be asked to roll Nature when building a campfire or tracking the thief who ransacked your campsite.

Soul Skills

Liar

Liar represents your ability to invent untrue things and convince others of them. You may be asked to roll Liar when convincing a shopkeeper that the junk you are selling them is actually very valuable, or when you are trying to bluff your way past some guards. You may also be asked to roll Liar when forging a letter, or when giving insincere flattery.

<u>Wild Empathy</u>

Wild Empathy represents your ability to understand and communicate intent to wild creatures. You may be asked to roll Wild Empathy when taming a giant rat, or when convincing a wolf to back down. You may also be asked to roll Wild Empathy when identifying the motives of a cockatrice that set fire to a village, or when trying to understand the rustling of a plant creature.

<u>Social Instinct</u>

Social Instinct represents your ability to understand others and discern their motives and truthfulness. You may be asked to roll Social Instinct when deciding whether the person who hired you to steal back their jewels is lying about what happened, or when playing a gambling game that includes bluffing. You may also be asked to roll Social Instinct when deciding how to most quickly evacuate a room full of people, or when spending some time picking up on local culture.

Tip: Though it is referred to as an 'instinct', Social Instinct is a skill which can be learned through application and study. For some characters this will come naturally over time, while for others this may be the result of deliberate learning. Both are equally valid.

<u>Perform</u>

Perform represents your ability to put on a show. You may be asked to roll Perform when filling in for an actor in a play, or when busking with a lute on the street. You may also be asked to roll Perform when you read a stirring speech to a crowd or when you are dancing with a noble.

<u>Create</u>

Create represents your ability to make art or craft something new. You may be asked to roll Create when making a painting or knitting a jumper. You may also be asked to roll Create when writing a story or inventing a new piece of technology.

PROFICIENCIES: CHOOSING WHAT MAKES YOU SPECIAL

In addition to your traits and skills, characters in *Kin* have proficiencies. These are special actions a character can take that use up Energy Points (EP). A character may use a proficiency any time they have the required Energy Points and Action Points (AP) to do so. Proficiencies bear a resemblance and even overlap with many Traits, but while Traits are inherited, Proficiencies are learned.

A character may choose any proficiency they fit the prerequisites for so long as they have a Proficiency Point to spend. There are no other restrictions than those listed under the proficiency.

Unlike Trait Points and Skill Points, Proficiency Points may be saved up to spend at a later date. They can only be spent at Level Up, however.

Proficiencies fall into 3 main categories: Spells (Magic), Moves (Physical), and Plays (Social).

See <u>Proficiencies: Spells</u>, <u>Proficiencies: Moves</u>, and <u>Proficiencies: Plays</u> for more information.

BACKGROUND: CHOOSING WHERE YOU CAME FROM

Choosing your background is an important step in character creation because it requires you to begin to think of your character in terms of their story. For this reason, in *Kin*, background is not a mechanical step.

In order to play your character, you need to know what has shaped them at the point the story starts. What motivates them? What will they find the most challenging to overcome, and why? And something too important to overlook: what is their relationship with other members of the party, and what binds them to this group?

To begin shaping your character, try answering the questions below. Short answers are fine; in-depth answers might provide detail, but quick answers provide flexibility, which is just as important.

Who are you?

Think about your personality. Your likes and dislikes. What makes you too angry to be sensible? What makes you trust someone? What are you afraid of? And why, do you think, any of this is the case?

What's your story so far?

Everyone's story starts somewhere. Where are you from? What is your family like? How did you end up here at the start of the campaign? What have you overcome to make it this far? What is something from your past that might come up again?

What do you want now?

There has to be something motivating you, driving you on in the story. What is it — an achievement, an object, someone's approval? Are you seeking to learn? And what will it mean to you if you get what you want?

What's stopping you from getting it?

We all have obstacles in our way. Why is it that you haven't achieved your goal already? Is it just a matter of time and dedication, or are there more barriers in your way? Why do you want it even though it is challenging to get?

What's your relationship with the other characters in your party?

Your history and chemistry with the other characters is incredibly important as it will shape every interaction in the group. Is there a member of the party you are particularly close with? Do you share a history with any of them? Is there anyone you find difficult — and why do you remain in the group in spite of it?

Your goal here is to build a fulfilling and convincing group dynamic more than to create conflict. Ultimately, you want your character to get on well in the group and be able to bond with everyone in it, even if it's a bit rocky along the way.

What languages do you speak?

In addition to a Kin language (Fey, Astral, or Voidspeech), your character will know the language of where they grew up.

The languages are as follows:

- Mistembran (Mistembra)
- Urodon (various dialects of Oroxx Archipelago)
- Maluxi, Vett, Illindi, Qaran (all of Fendenmount)
- Solish (Sola Dun, Ser Vissa, and Vonna-dolar)
- Rox (Axtrn, Ixi, Munaxis, and Voidenfar)

Tip: There is no common language in *Kin*, so players may want to co-ordinate, or the GM may wish to give all players the language of the country they are playing in, in addition to any background languages.

DEFENCE

Defence represents your basic ability to withstand or avoid an attack. Your starting Defence unless modified by a Trait or Proficiency (such as one that allows you to wear armour) is 10. This is the most common Defence in the world, and most other creatures and characters you encounter will have a Defence of 10.

When you are attacked by an enemy, they will make their Attack Roll (Weapon Die + Fate Die) versus your Defence. If their total roll exceeds your Defence, you will be dealt a Wound. If their total roll equals or is less than your Defence, you have successfully avoided harm.

∞ PROFICIENCIES: SPELLS

℘ SPELLS

Magical Source

Spells are unique among proficiencies in that they are magical. Magic has many sources, and every time a character learns a new magical proficiency, they learn to power it from a particular source.

Sources are for role-playing purposes only, but source is important in how it interacts with the world. Some people use only one source, specialising and deepening their connection. Others draw from multiple sources, learning all there is to offer.

Magic comes from many places and many planes, but the most common magical sources are as follows:

Arcane

All magic is arcane, but to draw from magic directly is unpredictable, dangerous, and frequently requires a large amount of study. Those who do so, most frequently referred to as wizards or mages, learn to do so through a more thorough grasp of magical theory and through more complex spell casting.

Arcane casters tend to draw more runes in their casting, specifying exactly what they require before they risk pulling from the source.

Nature

Magic saturates the world — the creatures, the plants, the earth, air, and water. Some magic users therefore choose to draw their magic through nature itself. This is one of the oldest sources of magic and is much safer as the natural world acts as a buffer to the arcane energies. Those who draw from nature are often referred to as witches.

Nature casters tend to draw fewer runes when casting but spend more time communing with nature and studying the natural world.

Soul

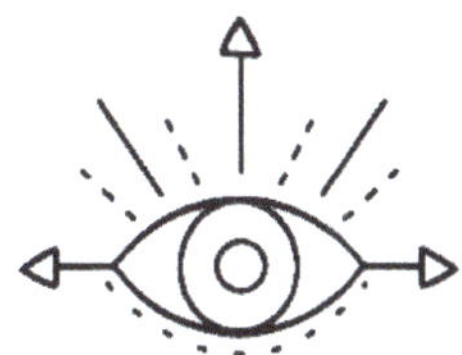

As magic saturates the world, it is no surprise that perhaps the oldest source of magic comes from within those who live in it. From the earliest days of humankind, people have been using their own souls to power spells, from storytellers making shapes in campfires to dancing and music being used in magical ceremonies of healing or celebration. Those who draw their power from their own souls are often referred to as bards.

Soul casters spend little time in magical study, substituting runes for music, dancing, and art, skills which they must develop alongside their magic.

Dedication

Sometimes magic is not learned, but awarded from those powerful enough to spare it. Such is the path of dedication. Those who pledge their service to magical beings in exchange for power are known by names as varied as the beings they serve. Some gain their proficiencies from gods, others from extraplanar entities.

Dedication casters do not need to learn their spells and may not use runes at all, but must work to build their connection with the one they serve if they intend to see their powers grow.

Spell List

Alterdimensional Extension

You are able to temporarily increase the interior dimensions of an object. This proficiency may be taken multiple times, increasing in power each time. This lasts 24 hours but can be maintained at the same EP cost for each 24 hour period, incurring no additional AP to maintain.

1 point: You are able to quadruple (x4) the interior dimensions of an object no larger than a basket ball.

2 points: You are able to sextuple (x6) the interior dimensions of an object no larger than a tent.

3 points: You are able to decuple (x10) the interior dimensions of an object no larger than a house.

4 points: You are able to permanently (up to x10) increase the interior dimensions of an object no larger than a house, until you choose to end the effect. This costs 15 EP.

Range: Close
EP per use: 1 (unless permanent)
AP per use: 1
Stat Req: Mind 3 (+2 per additional point)

Animate Rope

You are able to remotely control a rope with your mind, inducing it to tie or untie itself, to slither like a snake, to pull itself taut or coil itself neatly. The rope does not have enough force to crush, harm, or otherwise cause a wound, but if undetected it can bind and restrain, or trip up the unsuspecting.

Range: Long
EP: 1 per hour of use.
AP per use: 1
Stat Req: Mind 2

Arcane Sense

You are able to sense the presence of spells and enchantments even if they are hidden from sight. You may put multiple points into this proficiency. Increasing its effectiveness each time.

1 point: You can sense that there is a spell or enchantment nearby and can pinpoint its source.

2 points: You can identify the general purpose of the magic (protection, harm, elemental energy, healing, etc) but not the specifics of how it works.

3 points: You can identify the specific effect of the spell or enchantment and how to either trigger or disable it (though this does not mean that you are capable of either).

Range: Nearby
EP: 3 per 10 minutes of use
AP per use: 1
Stat Req: Mind 3 (+3 per additional point)

Arcane Packbeast

You create a translucent pill-shaped trunk that follows in your footsteps. You can make it more or less opaque (even invisible) and it levitates a few feet above the ground and can smoothly take stairs or cross any gap you can. If you are flying, it can fly behind you. The arcane packbeast can carry up to three times your weight, either on its surface or within it once opened. It can only be opened by the caster.

Range: Close
EP: 1 per hour of use.
AP per use: 1
Stat Req: Mind 1

Blink

You can teleport a certain distance in any direction without passing through the intervening spaces. This is limited by your line of sight. You may take this proficiency multiple times with the following progression:

1 point: Range is Nearby.

2 points: Range is Long.

3 points: Range is Far.

Range: (see description)
EP per use: 3
AP per use: 1
Stat Req: Mind 3 (+3 per additional point)

Charm Mind

You enforce your will on another creature, overwhelming their defences. The target has the chance to make a Mind Check to resist the spell (Mind stat + Fate die) against your Mind stat + 10 and on a success, they suffer no effects and are aware that you attempted to dominate their mind. Charm Mind can have a number of effects depending on how many points you have put into this proficiency. The target may repeat this check each hour but will not be aware after an initial success.

You may take this proficiency multiple times, increasing its effectiveness each time.

**NOTE: Charm Mind and any mind-altering spells are considered illegal, evil, and taboo in most of Vanthis, so it can be difficult to learn. Discuss with your GM if you want to learn.*

1 point: You can minorly influence the target's emotions, causing them to become calm, angry, or friendly. While thus charmed, they are more likely to heed your words (dependent on a successful related Skill Check). The target will be **unaware** *that you have cast this spell on them after the effect ends. The effect will immediately end once the target is a Long distance away. This costs 3 EP per hour.*

2 points: You can directly command the target and they will heed your words and do as ordered, so long as they are capable and it doesn't cause a wound to them or someone they care about. For example, you could tell them to leave, to sleep, to dance, or to give you all *their possessions, and they would do so. The target will be **aware** that you have cast this spell on them after the effect ends and may grow hostile. The effect will immediately end once the target is a Long distance away. This costs 5 EP per hour.*

*3 points: You can command the target to do anything and they will heed your words and do as ordered without restriction, even attempting things they are not capable of. The target will be **aware** that you have cast this spell on them after the effect ends and may grow hostile. Distance will not cause this effect to end. This costs 10 EP per hour.*

Note: you may use this proficiency at a lower power level and it will cost the same as it would at the lower level (eg if you have 3 points in Charm Mind but you only want to influence the target's emotions, it will cost 3 EP per hour instead of 10).

Range: Nearby
EP: (see description)
AP per use: 1
Stat Req: Mind 2, Soul 2 (+2 Mind per additional point)

Control Elements

You create or control up to a fist-sized amount of elemental energy and manipulate it, changing its shape, state, and colour, or vanishing it. To attack with that element (for air: lightning, for water: ice), you use a d4 as your Weapon Die for the Attack Check and it does the same damage type as the element used.

You may take this proficiency multiple times, choosing a different element each time. The options are: fire, water, air, and earth.

Range: Long
EP per use: 2
AP per use: 1
Stat Req: Mind 2

Creature Sense

You are able to sense the presence of creatures and can pinpoint their source even if you cannot see them.

1 point: You can sense that there are creatures nearby and in which direction, but you cannot tell more. Range is Long. EP is 2 per hour.

2 points: The Range becomes Far. EP is 3 per hour.

3 points: You can identify specific details of the creatures you sense, including what they are, any immunities, or natural abilities. If they are familiar to you, you will know who they are specifically. EP is 5 per hour.

Note: you may use this proficiency at a lower power level and it will cost the same as it would at the lower level (eg if you have 3 points in Creature Sense but you only want to know IF there are creatures within a Long range, it will cost 2 EP per hour instead of 5).

Range: (see description)
EP per use: (see description)
AP per use: 1
Stat Req: Mind 2, Soul 2 (+2 Mind per additional point)

Elemental Strike

You create or control up to a horse-sized amount of elemental energy and manipulate it, changing its shape, state, and colour, or vanishing it. To attack with that element (for air: lightning, for water: ice), you use a d8 as your Weapon Die for the attack and it does the same damage type as the element used.

The element may also be shaped into a wall, cage, or similar shapes such as might impede movement. In that case, the attack does damage only when touched.

You may take this proficiency multiple times, choosing a different element each time. The options are: fire, water, air, and earth.

Range: Long
EP per use: 10
AP per use: 2
Stat Req: Mind 5

Healer's Touch

You touch someone, filling them with healing energies that can close wounds and have a number of other healing effects. You may take this proficiency multiple times, increasing its power with each point.

1 point: On touch, you can heal up to 1 Wound. 2 EP per use.

2 points: On touch, you can cure poison, sickness, or other similar effects. 3 EP per use.

3 points: On touch, you can heal up to 3 Wound. 5 EP per use.

Note: you may use this proficiency at a lower power level and it will cost the same as it would at the lower level (eg if you have 3 points in Healer's Touch but you only want to heal 1 Wound, it will cost 2 EP per use instead of 5).

Range: Close
EP per use: (see description)
AP per use: 1
Stat Req: Soul 2, Mind 1 (+2 Soul per additional point)

Healing Wind

You direct healing energy from a distance, healing all those it touches.

1 point: You can heal one creature up to 1 Wound. 5 EP per use.

2 points: You can heal one creature up to 2 Wound or two creatures 1 Wound. 7 EP per use.

3 points: You can heal one creature up to 3 Wound or up to 3 creatures 3 Wound between them. 9 EP per use.

4 points: You can heal one creature up to 5 Wound or up to 5 creatures 5 Wound between them. 11 EP per use.

5 points: You can heal all creatures of your choosing within a Long distance 1 Wound. 15 EP per use.

Note: you may use this proficiency at a lower power level and it will cost the same as it would at the lower level (eg if you have 3 points in Healing Wind but you only want to heal 1 Wound, it will cost 5 EP per use instead of 10).

Range: Long
EP per use: (see description)
AP per use: 2
Stat Req: Soul 3, Mind 2 (+1 Soul per additional point)

Illumination

You can create or control magical lights up to the size of your fist, choosing their level of brightness, shape, and moving them with or without touching them. Lighting up a Close or Nearby distance costs 0 EP.

You may take this proficiency multiple times, increasing its power with each point.

1 point: You can create a light bright enough to adequately light up a Long distance. 1 EP per use, 0 AP.

2 points: You may spend 3 EP and 1 AP to create a light bright enough to blind those Nearby to it for 1 round. You may maintain this effect at the same rate of 3 EP per round, but it does not incur additional AP to maintain.

Range: Long
EP per use: (see description)
AP per use: (see description)
Stat Req: Mind 2 (+1 per additional point)

Illusion

You create illusions, tricks of light and the mind which create or change visuals but not physical reality. You may take this proficiency multiple times, increasing its power and function each time.

1 point: you can create small, simple illusions, such as a hologram the size of a map, making the sound of a wolf howl nearby, or changing the colour of your eyes. You can create sounds OR visuals, but not both at the same time. You must actively control and concentrate on the illusion. 0 EP per hour of use and 1 AP per round.

2 points: you can create more moderately complex illusions, such as disguising a door as the wall behind it, an illusory creature the size of a bear, or turning someone invisible. You can create sounds AND visuals but the illusions will be revealed on close inspection or touch. You must actively control and concentrate on the illusion. 3 EP per hour of use and 1 AP per round.

3 points: you can create truly complex illusions such as disguising someone as someone else, changing the appearance of an entire room, or creating an illusory creature the size of a dragon. You can create sounds AND visuals and the illusions will stand up to close inspection and touch, fooling the mind of the person. You must actively control and concentrate on the illusion. 5 EP per hour of use and 1 AP per use.

4 points: You can create scripted illusions that will act without supervision, provided you designate the script. So you can create an illusory wolf that will only appear when someone enters a designated area and then will howl and snarl at them. You can create an illusory person that will pretend to die when attacked. You do not have to actively control or concentrate on the illusion to maintain it. 7 EP per hour of use and 1 AP per round.

5 points: Illusions cost half EP (rounded up, for a minimum of 1 EP) to cast.

Note: you may use this proficiency at a lower power level and it will cost the same as it would at the lower level (eg if you have 3 points in Illusion but you only want to change the colour of your eyes, it will cost 1 EP per hour instead of 5).

Range: Long
EP: (see description)
AP: 1 per round
Stat Req: Mind 2, Soul 2 (+ 1 Soul per each additional point)

Nature's Voice

You forge a connection to nature, which you use to communicate with it. For one hour you can communicate with either plants or animals that would not normally be capable of understanding language. They understand you perfectly, but cannot communicate back verbally.

Their response is limited by the natural behaviours and vocalisations available to that creature (eg a dog might bark and show you the way. A plant may be capable of rustling or leaning in a direction; a magical plant might be able to grow or move.)

You may need to succeed on a relevant Skill Check (such as Threaten, Convince, or Liar) in order to gain their assistance; the spell does not compel the creature or plant to help.

You may take this proficiency twice, choosing either Animals or Plants each time.

Range: Long

EP per use: 3

AP per use: 1

Stat Req: Mind 2, Soul 4

Polymorph

You can magically transform yourself into a non-humanoid creature you have seen or are familiar with through other means. Your new shape has the natural abilities of that creature, and has a separate pool of Wound. When the creature has been fully wounded, you revert to your normal shape and the level of Wound you had prior to transforming. It has restrictions based on the power level of the proficiency. You may choose to revert at any time but cannot otherwise cast spells.

You may take this proficiency multiple times, increasing the proficiency's power each time.

1 point: You can become any non-flying, non-aquatic creature the size of a cat or smaller, and you can sustain 1 Wound while in that shape. You cannot do enough damage to cause a Wound. Costs 2 EP per hour of use. Costs 1 AP to cast.

2 points: You can become any non-flying, non-aquatic creature the size of a wolf, and you can sustain 1 Wound while in that shape. You can attack with d4 as your Weapon Die. Costs 3 EP per hour of use. Costs 1 AP to cast.

3 points: You can now become aquatic creatures. The other rules still apply.

4 points: You can become any non-flying creature the size of a bear and you can sustain 2 Wound while in that shape. You can attack with d6 as your Weapon Die. Costs 4 EP per hour of use. Costs 2 AP to cast.

5 points: You can now become a flying creature. The other rules still apply.

6 points: You can become any creature the size of a rhino, and you can sustain 3 Wound while in that shape. You can attack with d6 as your Weapon Die. Costs 6 EP per hour of use. Costs 3 AP to cast.

7 points: You can become any creature the size of a dragon, and you can sustain 3 Wound while in that shape. You can attack with d8 as your Weapon Die. Costs 7 EP per hour of use. Costs 3 AP to cast.

8 points: All previous levels cost 2 less EP per hour of use (for a minimum of 1 EP). You can polymorph other creatures than yourself. If they are unwilling, they must succeed on a Mind Check (Mind stat + Fate die) against your Mind stat + 10 to resist.

Note: you may use this proficiency at a lower power level and it will cost the same as it would at the lower level (eg if you have 4 points in Polymorph but turn into a cat, you can only sustain 1 Wound and cannot cause Wound, but it only costs 2 EP per hour of use.)

EP per hour of use: (see description)
AP per use: (see description)
Stat Req: Mind 3, Soul 2 (+1 to Mind per additional point)

Scry

You are able to magically view a known person, object, or location using anything sufficiently reflective or cloudy (examples of appropriate objects to scry through include water, crystal balls, or fire). You can see the immediate surroundings of the person or object (a Close distance) or see the location in full from an appropriate distance which may hide details. You can hear what you would hear from the subject's POV. Scrying is not instantaneous and takes place in real-time.

EP per hour: 5
AP per use: 1 (and cannot take other actions while scrying)
Stat Req: Mind 3, Soul 2

Seal

You are able to seal a mundane portal capable of closing (eg a door, a window, a hatch) or closeable object (eg a bag, a chest, a wardrobe). This spell essentially freezes the closable element in place, does not require a locking mechanism, and cannot be unlocked by traditional means.

You may also use this spell to unseal an object or portal sealed in this manner. The object or portal remains sealed until the caster either chooses to end the spell or it is unsealed by another caster.

Range: Close

EP per use: 2

AP per use: 1

Stat Req: Mind 3

Telekinesis

You can magically manipulate any object within sight and range that you would be able to freely lift with one hand. This includes manipulating parts of a larger object. You cannot manipulate it with enough force to cause a Wound (eg by throwing it at someone).

You may take this proficiency multiple times, increasing the power of the proficiency each time.

1 point: Range is Nearby, EP per use is 0.

2 points: Range is Long, EP per use is 1.

3 points: Range is Long, EP per use is 2, capable of causing a Wound (attack uses d4 for Weapon Die)

4 points: Range is Long, EP per use is 3 capable of causing a Wound (attack uses d6 for Weapon die), capable of lifting something up to your own body weight.

5 points: Range is Long, EP per use is 4, capable of causing a Wound (attack uses d8 for Weapon die) capable of lifting something up to the weight of a horse.

Note: you may use this proficiency at a lower power level and it will cost the same as it would at the lower level (eg if you have 4 points in Telekinesis but you want to lift something Nearby that you would be able to freely lift with one hand and do not intend to attack with it, it will only cost 0 EP).

Range: (see description)

EP per use: (see description)

AP per use: 1

Stat Req: Mind 2 (+2 per additional point)

Telepathy

You are able to speak directly into the mind of any creature within sight or whom you know to be Close. If they are capable of speech, they understand your words, regardless of language. If they wish to ignore you, they can make a Mind Check (Mind stat + Fate die) against your Mind stat + 10 and on a success, they no longer hear your telepathy for the next hour.

Range: within sight
EP per use: 1
AP per use: 0
Stat Req: Mind 5, Soul 3

Truthsayer

You create a circle in which lies cannot be spoken, and all within will feel a strong compulsion to speak the truth when questioned — including the caster. This effect can be resisted by each it effects with a Mind Check (Mind stat + Fate die) against your Mind stat + 10 and on a success, they can lie freely and feel no compulsion.

Range: a Close circle around the caster
EP per use: 5
AP per use: 2
Stat Req: Mind 5, Soul 5

Whisperwind

You speak into a shell, cup, or similar-sized concave item and your voice is carried to a familiar entity of your choice who is on the same plane as you, who hears the message as if it is a voice carried on the wind. They can reply in kind.

Range: same plane
EP per use: 1 per minute
AP per use: 1
Stat Req: Mind 3, Soul 3

౭ PROFICIENCIES: MOVES

ℬ MOVES

Move List

Armoured

You are able to comfortably wear and take advantage of increasingly heavy and protective armour. You may take this proficiency multiple times, increasing its effectiveness with each point.

1 point: You are able to wear light, flexible armours such as leather, padded cloth, or leaf armour. Your Defence is +2 while wearing this armour.

2 points: You are able to wear medium, protective armours such as bamboo, fae mail, or chitin armour. Your Defence is +3 while wearing this armour.

3 points: You are able to wear heavy, protective armours such as chain mail, plate, or dragon scale. Your Defence is +5 while wearing this armour.

Stat Req: Body 2 (+1 per additional point)

Balancing Act

You are unusually skilled at keeping your balance.

Note: You may take this proficiency multiple times, choosing a different effect each time. This proficiency does not stack: each point applies to a different situation. You may take these points out of order.

1 point: You may spend 3 EP to gain +3 on an Agility check to climb or catch yourself.

2 points: You may spend 3 EP to gain +3 on an Agility check for a feat of balance or acrobatics.

3 points: You may spend 3 EP to gain +5 on any Agility check, regardless of the circumstance. Cannot be taken until all previous points have been taken.

EP per use: (see description)
AP per use: 1
Stat Req: Body 2 (+2 Body per additional point)

Clean Sweep

You sweep the legs right out from under your opponent. They must spend 1 AP on their next turn standing up again. You may take this proficiency multiple times, increasing its effectiveness each time.

1 point: You can Clean Sweep one opponent standing Close. Costs 2 EP.

2 points: You can Clean Sweep two opponents standing Close. Costs 3 EP.

3 points: You can Clean Sweep three opponents standing Close. Costs 5 EP.

Note: you may use this proficiency at a lower power level and it will cost the same as it would at the lower level (eg if you have 3 points in Clean Sweep but you want to Clean Sweep only 1 opponent you, it will only cost 2 EP).

Range: Close
EP per use: (see description)
AP per use: 1
Stat Req: Body 5 (+1 per additional point)

Dodgy

You forgo heavier armours, looking to capitalise on speed instead. While you are wearing no armour or armour classed as light armour, you are harder to hit. You may take this proficiency multiple times, increasing its effectiveness with each point. Modifiers stack with Armour Adept when wearing Light Armour only.

1 point: You are good at turning your body to avoid the worst of a blow. Your Defence is +1 while wearing no armour or light armour.

2 points: You are able to roll, flip, and dodge to avoid the worst of a blow. Your Defence is +2 while wearing no armour or light armour.

3 points: You are so quick on your feet that it is difficult to land a critical blow. When a critical attack is rolled against you, your attacker must make a Body Check versus your Body +10. If they fail the check, the attack is no longer critical and does not do extra Wound.

Stat Req: Body 2 (+1 per additional point)

Hardy

You have trained yourself to be more physically tough and endurant and to withstand greater pain. You can therefore take more Wound before becoming incapacitated.

1 point: Your base total Wound you can withstand is increased to 4.

2 points: Your base total Wound you can withstand is increased to 5.

Stat Req: Body 7 (+5 Body per additional point)

Keen Senses

You have trained your senses to be particularly keen. You are able to make full use of sight, smell, taste, hearing, and touch for increased perception in appropriate circumstances. When you make a Search check, you may call on this proficiency to reroll the skill die and take the higher roll.

EP per use: 2
Stat Req: Body 3, Mind 2

Lauded Locksmith

You are a talented locksmith, able to crack locks and disable traps with speed and efficiency.

Note: You may take this proficiency multiple times, choosing a different effect each time. This proficiency does not stack: each point applies to a different situation. You may take these points out of order.

1 point: You may spend 3 EP to gain +3 on a Thievery check to pick a non-magical lock.

2 points: You may spend 3 EP to gain +3 on a Thievery check to check for or disable a trap.

3 points: You may spend 3 EP to gain +3 on a Thievery check to lock or trap something, or reset a previous lock or trap.

4 points: You may spend 3 EP to gain +5 on any Thievery check to do with locks or traps, regardless of the circumstance. Cannot be taken until all previous points are taken.

Stat Req: Body 3, Mind 2 (+1 Body per additional point)

Light-footed

You can briefly move with extreme quietness, barely making a whisper of sound even in the noisiest terrain. You may activate this proficiency to gain +5 on a relevant Stealth check.

EP per use: 3
Stat Req: Body 5

Looming Presence

You loom impressively, looking physically intimidating. You may activate this proficiency to gain a +5 bonus to a Threaten or relevant social check depending on context.

EP per use: 3
Stat Req: Body 3, Soul 2

Meditative Recovery

You are a master of meditation. When resting, you recover EP at twice the normal rate (so 2EP per hour of rest, and 4 hours for a full rest.)

Stat Req: Body 5, Mind 5

Melee Specialist

You are well-trained for melee combat. You hit harder and smarter, for more damage, and can use a variety of weapons. You may take this proficiency multiple times, increasing its effectiveness each time.

1 point: You can handle heavier and more complex weapons. You can now use melee weapons other than daggers and staffs. Your weapon die is a d4.

2 points: Your weapon die is now a d6.

3 points: You can now use a shield and block. When someone rolls an attack against you, you may spend 3 EP to attempt to block with your shield or weapon, reducing the damage by 1 Wound.

4 points: Your weapon die is now a d8.

5 points: You can now dual wield appropriate one-handed weapons (dagger, swords, etc). When you make an attack, you may choose to spend 3 EP to make it a dual wield attack. Roll the weapon die twice for your Attack Check and take the higher roll.

6 points: You can now parry. When someone makes a melee attack against you, you may spend 3 EP to parry. You and your attacker make opposing Body Checks (Body + Fate die). Whoever rolls higher takes the Wound of the original attack.

Stat Req: Body 1 (+1 per additional point)

Mighty Leap

You take a mighty leap, jumping far further than you normally would. In a leap, or series of leaps, you move a Long distance for only 1 AP and leap over creatures and objects in the intervening space.

EP per use: 3
AP per use: 1
Stat Req: Body 6

Practiced Pickpocket

You are especially skilled at taking things unnoticed from one's person, being exceptionally light-fingered and aware of the focus of others.

Note: You may take this proficiency multiple times, choosing a different effect each time. This proficiency does not stack: each point applies to a different situation. You may take these points out of order.

1 point: You know how to seize opportunity. You may spend 3 EP to gain +3 on a Thievery check to pickpocket someone who is distracted or unaware of your presence.

2 points: The real trick isn't taking; it's giving. You may spend 3 EP to gain +3 on a Thievery check to 'reverse pickpocket' someone and plant an item on their person.

3 points: If you're close enough to touch, it's already too late. You may spend 3 EP to gain +3 on a Thievery check to pickpocket someone you are already touching, even in plain sight.

4 points: You're as light-fingered as they come. You may spend 3 EP to gain +5 on any Thievery check to pickpocket, regardless of the circumstance. Cannot be taken until all other points are taken.

Stat Req: Body 3, Soul 2 (+1 Body per additional point)

Ranged Specialist

You are well-trained for ranged combat. You have better aim and swifter shots, and you can use a variety of weapons. You may take this proficiency multiple times, increasing its effectiveness each time.

1 point: You can now use ranged weapons, including bows, throwing knives, etc. Your weapon die is a d4. Ranged weapons can only be used at a distance of Nearby or farther.

2 points: Your weapon die is now a d6.

3 points: You can now use ranged weapons at a Close distance, stabbing them with the projectile (eg arrow, knife etc) or beating them with the weapon itself. When attacking someone at a Close distance with a ranged weapon or ranged weapon's projectile, you use a d4 for your weapon die regardless of the weapon and points in this or other proficiencies.

4 points: Your weapon die is now a d8.

5 points: You can now loose two projectiles at once. When you make a ranged attack, you may choose to spend 3 EP to make it a double attack. Roll the weapon die twice for your Attack Check and take the higher roll.

6 points: You can now do a volley of projectiles. When you make a ranged attack, you may choose to spend 5 EP to make it a volley. You may roll up to 3 weapon dice with your attack, each representing a different projectile. Each hit does 1 Wound (only one may be Critical, and do an additional Wound), for a maximum of 3 Wound (or 4 if one is Critical). These cannot be split across opponents.

Stat Req: Body 1 (+1 per additional point)

Surge of Speed

*You immediately feel a powerful surge of speed and are able to move much more quickly than you normally would. Movement costs 1 less AP per range with a minimum of 0. You can also Sprint for an additional 5 EP which will move you a Far distance for only 1 AP.**

**does not stack with the Speedy Trait.*

EP per use: 3 (+5 to sprint)
Stat Req: Body 10

Surge of Strength

You immediately feel a powerful surge of strength and are briefly able to lift something many times heavier than you normally would. This can also be used in non-lifting contexts (such as arm-wrestling, tug of war, etc). You may activate this proficiency to gain +5 on a relevant Endurance check.

EP per use: 3
AP per round: 1
Stat Req: Body 5

Tumble

You carefully control your landing, rolling to spread and reduce the worst of the damage.

You may take this proficiency multiple times, increasing its effectiveness each time.

1 point: You can ignore up to 1 Wound of fall damage (eg a fall that might break a bone).

2 points: You can ignore up to 2 Wound of fall damage (eg a fall that might cause internal bleeding).

3 points: You can ignore up to 3 Wound of fall damage (eg a fall that might knock you unconscious).

Stat Req: Body 5 (+1 per additional point)

Wallclimb

You can climb directly up or down vertical surfaces provided they can take your weight. Climbing does not require a Skill Check when this proficiency is used.

EP per use: 3
Stat Req: Body 5

Weapon Bounce

You expertly attack by throwing a shield or heavy weapon such that it bounces back into your hand. This attack automatically hits. When you use this proficiency, roll a Fate die: on a 1, there is a critical failure and the attack still does a Wound, but the weapon does not return to your hand.

Note: Weapon bounce does not apply to ranged weapons or weapons normally used as projectiles (eg you cannot Weapon Bounce your dagger).

Range: Long
EP per use: 3
AP per use: 1
Stat Req: Body 6, Mind 2

Whirlwind

You make a spinning attack, striking all the enemies surrounding you. This attack hits up to 3 enemies for 1 Wound each.

Range: Close
EP per use: 5
AP per use: 2
Stat Req: Body 10

ഊ PROFICIENCIES: PLAYS

ಬ PLAYS

Play List

Assuming Airs

You project confident nobility or celebrity and act as if you expect your every command to be followed. You may activate this proficiency to gain +5 on any Liar or Convince check where you are claiming high status.

EP per use: 3
Stat Req: Soul 5

Alchemical Genius

You are a skilled and talented alchemist with a thorough understanding of alchemical principles. Consequently, you can make potions that are a little more potent than most!

Note: You may take this proficiency multiple times, choosing a different effect each time. This proficiency does not stack: each point applies to a different situation. You may take these points out of order.

1 point: You are reliable with the basics. Spend 3 EP to gain +3 on an Alchemy check to create a healing potion (restores 1 Wound) or energy potion (restores 5 EP).

2 points: You can craft potions with unusual effects. Spend 3 EP to gain +3 on an Alchemy check to create a potion using a new recipe with an effect other than healing or energy restoration.

3 points: Your potions are a little more potent than those crafted by others. When you successfully craft a healing potion, it heals 1 Wound more than normal. When you successfully craft an Energy potion, it restores 5 EP more than normal. Cannot be taken until all other points are taken.

EP per use: (see description)
Stat Req: Mind 3 (+3 Mind per additional point)

Clairvoyant

You are a little cannier than the average person, a little more in touch with fate and possibility. Once per full rest, before making a Skill Check or using another proficiency, you may activate this proficiency. If you do not like the immediate result of the Skill Check (think 1 minute of Narrative Mode or end of your turn in Action Mode, max), you may undo this action as if it never happened and do something else instead.

EP per use: 5
Stat Req: Soul 10

Creative Type

You are practiced in a particular craft or art form. You may activate this proficiency to gain +5 on any Create check involving that specific craft, instrument or art form. (Examples: knitting, painting, poetry, smithy, needle-felting, pottery, tinkering, etc.)

Note: You may take this proficiency multiple times, choosing a different craft or art form each time.

EP per use: 3
Stat Req: Soul 3

Creature Carer

You have a natural ability with wild things and non-speaking creatures, able to calm, befriend, and even command them.

Note: You may take this proficiency multiple times, choosing a different effect each time. This proficiency does not stack: each point applies to a different situation. You may take these points out of order.

1 point: You are able to calm frightened or enraged creatures. Spend 3 EP to gain +3 on a relevant Wild Empathy check to calm a hostile or scared creature.

2 points: You can use creature behaviour to get a better understanding of your environment or situation. Spend 3 EP to gain +3 on a relevant Wild Empathy check in the place of a Search check.

3 points: You can often convince creatures to help or guide you. Spend 3 EP to gain +5 on any Wild Empathy check, regardless of circumstances. Cannot be taken until all other points have been taken.

EP per use: (see description)
Stat Req: Soul 2, Body 1 (+3 Soul per additional point)

Crowd Gatherer

You project your voice, gaining the attention of all those in the vicinity and enticing them to come nearer. You are able to gather a crowd of non-hostile people and maintain it for as long as you keep talking and they do not perceive themselves to be in immediate danger.

EP per use: 3
Stat Req: Soul 7

Cryptid

You are fully capable of disappearing into the wilderness and thriving.

Note: You may take this proficiency multiple times, choosing a different effect each time. This proficiency does not stack: each point applies to a different situation. You may take these points out of order.

1 point: You are able to gather and prepare filling meals. Spend 3 EP to gain +3 on a relevant Nature check to feed yourself and others.

2 points: You can find or build a safe and comfortable shelter. Spend 3 EP to gain +3 on a relevant Nature check to shelter yourself and others.

3 points: You know the wilds better than anyone. Spend 3 EP to gain +5 on any Nature check, regardless of circumstances. Cannot be taken until all other points are taken.

EP per use: (see description)
Stat Req: Soul 2, Body 1 (+3 Soul per additional point)

Dicey

You have a knack for gambling, which always seems to go your way. They might be games of chance, but you don't leave it up to fate ...

When gambling, you may spend 1 EP to cheat on a particular round and re-roll the Fate die. However, your opponents may roll Social Instinct versus your Soul + 10 to detect your cheating.

EP per use: 1
Stat Req: Soul 1

Diplomat

You have poise and an earnest manner which makes you a skilled negotiator.

Note: You may take this proficiency multiple times, choosing a different effect each time. This proficiency does not stack: each point applies to a different situation. You may take these points out of order.

1 point: You have a calming effect on tense situations. Spend 3 EP to gain +3 on a relevant Convince check to ease tensions between two parties.

2 points: You can smoothly get the upper-hand in most deals. Spend 3 EP to gain +3 on a relevant Convince check to negotiate for better rewards or compensation.

3 points: You have a natural authority. Spend 3 EP to gain +5 on any Convince check, regardless of circumstances. Cannot be taken until all other points are taken.

Stat Req: Soul 2, Mind 1 (+3 Soul per additional point)

Educated

You are particularly educated or self-taught in a certain topic. You may activate this proficiency to gain +5 to Scholar checks for knowledge on this topic or to research it further. The topic may be broad and should not be covered by another skill (eg History, Politics, or Magical Theory are all good topics, but Animal Care is not as it is covered by either Wild Empathy or Nature depending on the circumstance).

Note: You may take this proficiency multiple times, choosing a different topic each time.

EP per use: 3
Stat Req: Mind 3

Empathic

You are great at reading people, even when they are trying to hide their true thoughts.

Note: You may take this proficiency multiple times, choosing a different effect each time. This proficiency does not stack: each point applies to a different situation. You may take these points out of order.

1 point: You know your friends better than anyone. Spend 3 EP to gain +3 on a relevant Social Instinct check when trying to read friends or allies.

2 points: You know the mind of your enemy. Spend 3 EP to gain +3 on a relevant Social Instinct check against someone openly opposed to you.

3 points: Even practiced liars struggle to get past you. Spend 3 EP to gain +5 on any Social Instinct check, regardless of the circumstance. Cannot be taken until all other points are taken.

EP per use: (see description)
Stat Req: Soul 2, Mind 1 (+3 Soul per additional point)

Flirtatious

You affect an easy charm and confident manner to win the affection and interest of your target. This proficiency may be taken multiple times, increasing its effectiveness each time. This proficiency does not stack; each point applies to a different situation.

1 point: You have an utterly charming wink. Spend 3 EP to gain +3 on a relevant Liar or Convince check to non-verbally flirt.

2 points: You can deliver the cheesiest pick-up lines with smouldering sincerity. Spend 3 EP to gain +3 on a relevant Liar or Convince check to flirt via pick-up line.

3 points: Even your attention can make people flustered. Spend 3 EP to gain +5 on any Liar or Convince check to flirt generally. Cannot be taken until all other points are taken.

Stat Req: Soul 2, Body 1 (+2 Soul per additional point)

Linguist

You are multi-lingual and fluent both in written and spoken form. Each time you take this proficiency, you may learn a new language. This proficiency is subject to GM approval, as you must have laid the groundwork for learning the new language either through study or through teaching.

Note: You may take this proficiency multiple times, choosing a different language each time.

Planar languages: Fey, Astral, Voidspeech (which are all inherently known by most with a dominant matching origin), Draconic

Human Languages: Mistembran (Mistembra), Urodon (various dialects of Oroxx Archipelago), Maluxi, Vett, Illindi, Qaran (all of Fendenmount), Solish (Sola Dun, Ser Vissa, and Vonna-dolar), Rox (Axtrn, Ixi, Munaxis, and Voidenfar)

Stat Req: Mind 2, Soul 1

Lucky Charm

You are luckier than most, and your allies reap the benefits of keeping you close. You may spend a Luck to allow a Nearby ally to re-roll a Fate 1 on any check. You may also spend a Luck to negate 1 Wound inflicted on a Nearby ally, turning it into a near miss. You may not use this proficiency to spend Luck on yourself in this manner.

Stat Req: Soul 5

Musician

You are practiced in a particular musical instrument. You may activate this proficiency to gain +5 on any Perform check involving that instrument. (Examples: flute, drums, singing, lyre, etc.)

Note: You may take this proficiency multiple times, choosing a different instrument each time.

EP per use: 2
Stat Req: Soul 3

Musical Number

You perform a cheering and inspiring song when your companions are low, re-energising them and showing them that things aren't as bad as they thought. Those within hearing you choose regain 5 EP each. Roll a Fate die: on a 15 or more, you and those within hearing you choose also reduce their Wound by 1.

Note: this proficiency may only be used once per full rest.

EP per use: 5
Stat Req: Soul 5

Observant

You are more aware of your surroundings than other people. This proficiency may be taken multiple times, increasing its effectiveness each time. This proficiency does not stack; each point applies to a different situation.

1 point: You are highly aware of your surroundings. Spend 3 EP to gain +3 on a Search check of your general area.

2 points: You are unusually good at sorting through objects. Spend 3 EP to gain +3 on a Search check when searching for specific items among many.

3 points: Very little gets past you. Spend 3 EP to gain +5 on any Search check.

Stat Req: Mind 2, Soul 1 (+3 Mind per additional point)

People Person

You're great at asking around and gathering information from strangers. You may activate this proficiency to gain +5 to any Convince or Liar checks when casually seeking information or rumours from strangers (such as at an inn, or asking around on the street), and people are more inclined to help.

EP per use: 2
Stat Req: Soul 3

Poker Face

You force your emotions down deep, hiding what you are truly feeling behind a still expression. You gain +3 on a relevant Liar check where you are keeping a blank face.

EP per use: 3
Stat Req: Soul 2, Mind 1

Ready for Anything

You plan ahead for even the most unlikely situations and always have just the item you need handy. Once per full rest, you may activate this proficiency to pull an item from your pack or personal belongings that will help you in your current situation, but which you may not have specifically listed. This item needs to feasibly exist and be available somewhere in the world, but can be somewhat rare or unlikely to be in your possession.

The item breaks or is lost after use and cannot be repaired. This cannot be used to increase your wealth and you cannot find a buyer for the item.

EP per use: 3
Stat Req: Soul 5, Mind 2

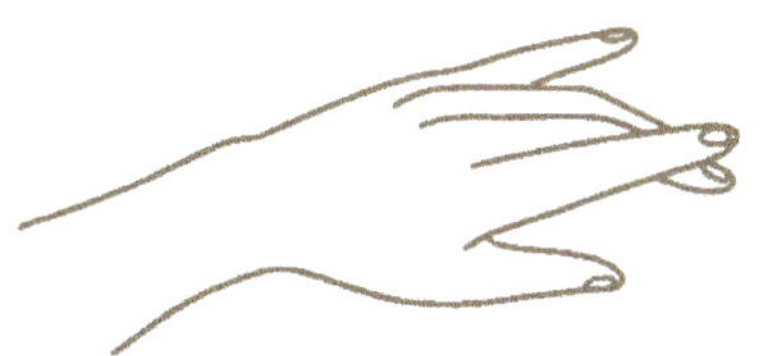

මි MONEY & INVENTORY MANAGEMENT

ဢ MONEY & INVENTORY MANAGEMENT

A part of TTRPG gameplay involves tracking money and items, so that the party knows what they have available to use and what they can afford to buy, from everything from a day's food to a magical item to a house. The main focus of *Kin* money and inventory management is: don't sweat the details.

MONEY

Money in *Kin* is unspecific. There's no need to track currency or exchange rates or set specific prices for items. Instead, *Kin* works on a Wealth Tier system, where player wealth is tracked in aggregate instead of specifically, and they are able to buy what they might reasonably be expected to afford within those tiers.

The Game Master will assign either the players or the party as a whole a Wealth Tier that they operate under. This can be increased over time (for example, if the party comes into a significant amount of money) or decreased (if the party spends or gives away a significant amount of money, or is robbed).

For roleplaying purposes, coins are the main currency of Vanthis.

Roundcoins, Tricoins, Boxcoins, and Hexcoins.

10 Roundcoins → 1 Tricoin

10 Tricoins → 1 Boxcoin

10 Boxcoins → 1 Hexcoin

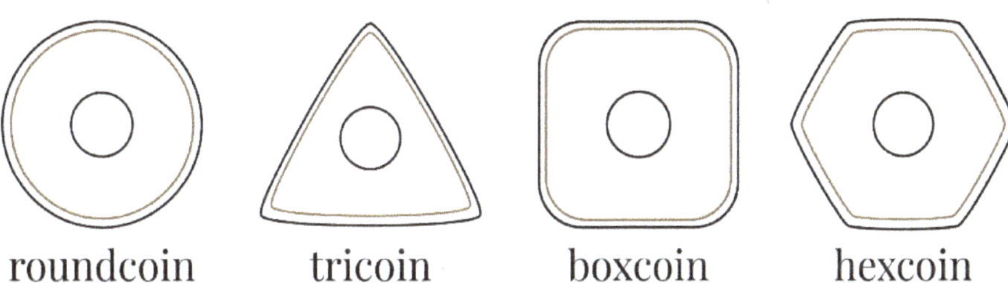

<table>
<tr><td colspan="3"><u>Wealth Tiers</u></td></tr>
<tr><td><u>Tier</u></td><td><u>Description</u></td><td><u>Can comfortably afford</u></td></tr>
<tr><td>Destitute</td><td>No money at all and likely no items of value.</td><td>Nothing. Will likely struggle to find food or shelter.</td></tr>
<tr><td>Poor</td><td>Struggling to make ends meet, no financial stability.</td><td>Can afford simple food and shelter, maybe the occasional treat.</td></tr>
<tr><td>Stable</td><td>Enough money that unexpected costs are not devastating.</td><td>Little concern for welfare. Can afford treats and save up for special things.</td></tr>
<tr><td>Wealthy</td><td>Able to sustain a luxurious lifestyle, more money than one person needs.</td><td>Able to splash out on luxury items and experiences without concern for cost.</td></tr>
<tr><td>Super Rich</td><td>Could not run out of money if actively trying to spend it all.</td><td>Nothing is unaffordable.</td></tr>
</table>

INVENTORY MANAGEMENT

Inventory management is slightly more detailed than money management but doesn't concern itself with weight or dimensions. Inventory management therefore operates under two key rules: the Rule of Sense, and the Rule of Available Storage.

Inventory: The Rule of Sense

The Rule of Sense is simple: if a character can sensibly be expected to carry the weight of something, they can. The Game Master and players may take different variables into account when deciding this: how high is the character's Body stat? How much are they already carrying? Is it too bulky to be easily carried? But ultimately, if you're sensible about it, the details don't really matter.

If the item is particularly large, heavy, or it is in some way unclear whether the character would be able to carry it, the Game Master will make a ruling on whether it can be carried or not (or whether they can temporarily carry it subject to an Endurance check, as the case may be) and that's the end of it.

Players should keep track of items they keep on their person, and at least one player should be put in charge of keeping track of items kept in group storage.

Inventory: The Rule of Available Storage

The Rule of Available Storage is all about where players can expect to store their items.

Typically, players will have a handful of simple storage options: store items on their person, store items in group storage, or store items in a location.

The Rule of Sense applies to each of these storage options; if it wouldn't fit in your pack and isn't easily transportable, it probably doesn't go on your person (and there's a reasonable limit to how much you would carry on your person). You can only store items in a location if you can get to that location. Group storage is more forgiving but has some limitations as well.

You might wonder: what is group storage, and how does it work? Simply put, all parties in *Kin* should be provided either at character creation or during their first session with some form of group storage. Group storage can carry far more items and is designed to be accessible to the whole party.

Details of the available options for group storage are in the table below:

Storage Type	Description	Limitations
Sack of Safekeeping	Magical sack enchanted with permanent Alterdimensional Extension, among other things, meaning its internal dimensions are far greater than its external dimensions would suggest. It doesn't increase in weight as more items are added. Some Sacks have additional enchantments such as only being accessible to certain persons, or requiring a password.	Can only hold items that can fit through the opening of the Sack. These items are relatively rare and therefore the group are unlikely to find more than one.
Horse and Cart	A cart drawn by a horse or other harnessable animal. Non-magical and can carry people as well as items. Relatively common to come by.	Limited by the size of the cart and the strength of the horse pulling it. Horse must be cared for. Large and unwieldy; will not be able to go everywhere the group will.
Potted Lillyteeth	A potted, carnivorous feykin plant whose 'mouth' opens as wide as a dinner plate. Lillyteeth however do not consume in the traditional sense; they collect. Things they consume go into a personal pocket plane. Lillyteeth will only allow certain people access and will painfully bite all others.	Must be watered and cared for and must have daily access to sunlight. Heavy. Can only hold items that can fit through its mouth. When it dies, all items are permanently lost. Relatively rare.

Some spells such as Alterdimensional Extension and Arcane Packbeast may have similar effects to Group Storage items, but are temporary and require EP to use. These spells are a simple way for a group to increase their storage.

Players may also be given a residence in which they can store items; however Group Storage refers to more portable storage as its purpose is for ease of gameplay.

MAGICAL ITEMS

Magical items (other than the Sack of Safekeeping) are not specifically listed in *Kin*. They are not especially common, other than a few specific cases (which will be listed below), and it is up to the Game Master to create these items and determine their effects and limitations, if they want to be used.

The most widely available magical items in *Kin* are as follows:

Magical armour: Typically, magical armour is resistant to being damaged or tarnished and can shift to fit the size and shape of the wearer.

Magical weapons: Like magical armour, magical weapons are difficult to destroy or even decay over time. Typically they have some additional effect (such as changing their damage type to Fire or producing light).

Potions: Potions are alchemical in nature. The most common potions are Healing Potions, which will typically restore 1 Wound when drunk, and Energy Potions, which will typically restore 5 EP when drunk. Other potions provide temporary resistance to certain damage types, or temporarily change the size of the drinker (for example, shrinking them to the size of a mouse or growing them to the size of a giant). There are also easily available gender balance potions which aid in medical transitioning and are custom prescribed. 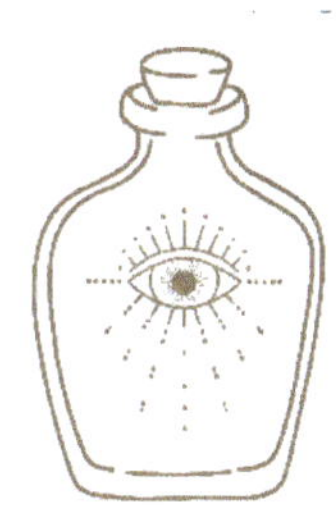

Disability aids: These come in a wide variety and are much more commonly available than any other kind of magical item. Examples of these are prosthetic limbs (some almost robotic, some made of pure energy powered by a ring or similar), enchanted canes and walking sticks, driftchairs (floating wheelchairs), and hexclimbers (spider-like wheelchairs).

THE WORLD OF VANTHIS

➷ THE WORLD OF VANTHIS

Vanthis, the primary world of the Associate Plane, is a land of magic, confluence, and contradiction. It may have once been a world not unlike Earth, but the long association with stranger, more magical planes has forever changed it, influencing its evolution and cultures.

THE PLANES

The Associate Plane is so known for its unusually close connection to other planes. It is likely that Vanthis is connected to a great many planes to varying degrees, but the three best known and most strongly connected planes are The Glamouring, The Astralar, and The Void Between Worlds. There are portals and gateways to other planes all across Vanthis — all temporary, all shifting and moving. Many opening in hidden and dark places.

The Fey Plane of The Glamouring

The Glamouring is a vast, ever-shifting wilderness of glowing forests, ember-like mountains, and sparkling seas. Its environments mimic those of the natural world, but are more vibrant. Larger, brighter, and more dangerous. It's a fluid world, shaped by the most powerful fey inhabitants, who can sing a forest into a treetop city, or reduce a mountain to a desert of rainbow sands.

The Fey themselves are beings of pure magic given form. Most appear to be animals, plants, or people, but more beautiful and strange than found in nature. The most powerful of them are shapeshifters themselves. They tend to live alone or in small family groups, suspicious of outsiders, and scheming against their neighbours. Their regard is capricious, and their ire is deadly, but they can be charmed by creative works, clever words, or their favourite past-time: making deals.

The Astral Plane of The Astralar

The Astralar is an endless star-studded seascape with its own natural laws. There is no air in those dark oceans, only different kinds of water. Floating among the sea and stars, surrounded by glittering trails of stardust, are asteroid-like structures hollow with crystalline caves and subterranean lakes.

The natural laws of The Astralar are thus: the thinnest water, that which feels almost like air, can be walked through and will not support the weight of non-astral creatures. The thicker water, that which resembles oceans and lakes, can be swum. Those waters are all connected, and entering a lake or pond can lead you anywhere in the Astral Plane, if you know how to do it. All water is breathable.

The inhabitants of The Astralar are swimming creatures varying in size from small, glowing astral fish to vast beings that could swallow a planet, drifting through the wider space-sea. And larger still. There are sentient and humanoid creatures in the Astralar, but they do not interact much with humans and little is known about their temperaments. Most are too large to even notice a human in their waters.

The Shadow Plane of The Void Between Worlds

 Little is known about The Void Between Worlds. It is theorised by some to be a single plane that seeps between the edges of all others, but yet others claim it is not one plane but many, each slightly different to its fellows. It is a subject of great research, complicated in that those that enter rarely come back, and those that do often come back changed.

What is certain is that it is a world of Shadow which normal human eyes cannot pierce. It contains a multitude of creatures, which emerge sometimes into the Associate Plane, most of them flying, all of them wreathed in shadow or possessing ghostly aspects. It is whipped by constant and terrible winds which can be heard even in the Associate Plane if a portal is near.

If there are people there, they are unknown to Vanthians. There are no records of native Void people, and Voidkin traits are considered to have originated at some point in the past through exposure to the Void rather than through inheritance, though Voidkin traits are as likely to be passed down to children as any Kin trait is.

VANTHIS AND THE ASSOCIATE PLANE

Vanthis is a broad world with influences even beyond its own plane. Due to the early influence of other planes on its development and the subsequent influx of all kinds of magic, Vanthis tends more toward a lower level of scientific technology than Earth, but it also has some surprising advances in magical technology, though these are not universal. It's a low-populated world where there are large expanses of untouched wilderness, partly due to the

Culturally, it is rare to find certain forms of bigotry common on Earth in Vanthis. In particular, the world is largely queernormative and learning one's own gender is common. Many wear magical runes, earrings, or other markers to denote their pronouns or gender. Sexism doesn't really exist except in some of the crueller cults, and never takes off. And racism never surfaced. Ableism is vanishingly rare, and most countries take accessibility seriously.

Humans are often kin of multiple kinds and are most often described by their most seemingly dominant kin. But since kin traits are not exclusively inherited and can have a number of sources, and since one kin can vary so wildly from the next even when related, there is almost universally no friction between different kinds of kin.

Magic is commonplace, as most people have small, innate magical abilities from birth. Magical tools and technology are slightly less common, and to be an active practitioner of magic usually takes a high level of dedication, practice, or study, which most do not do. There are often mages at the upper echelons of society, particularly in magic-rich countries such as those of the Mistembra Isles.

The study of arcane magic, such as is attributed to mages and wizards, is considered high-class; to practice magic where the source is nature, soul, or dedication is considered common and low-class in spite of its relative rarity. There are some exceptions to this.

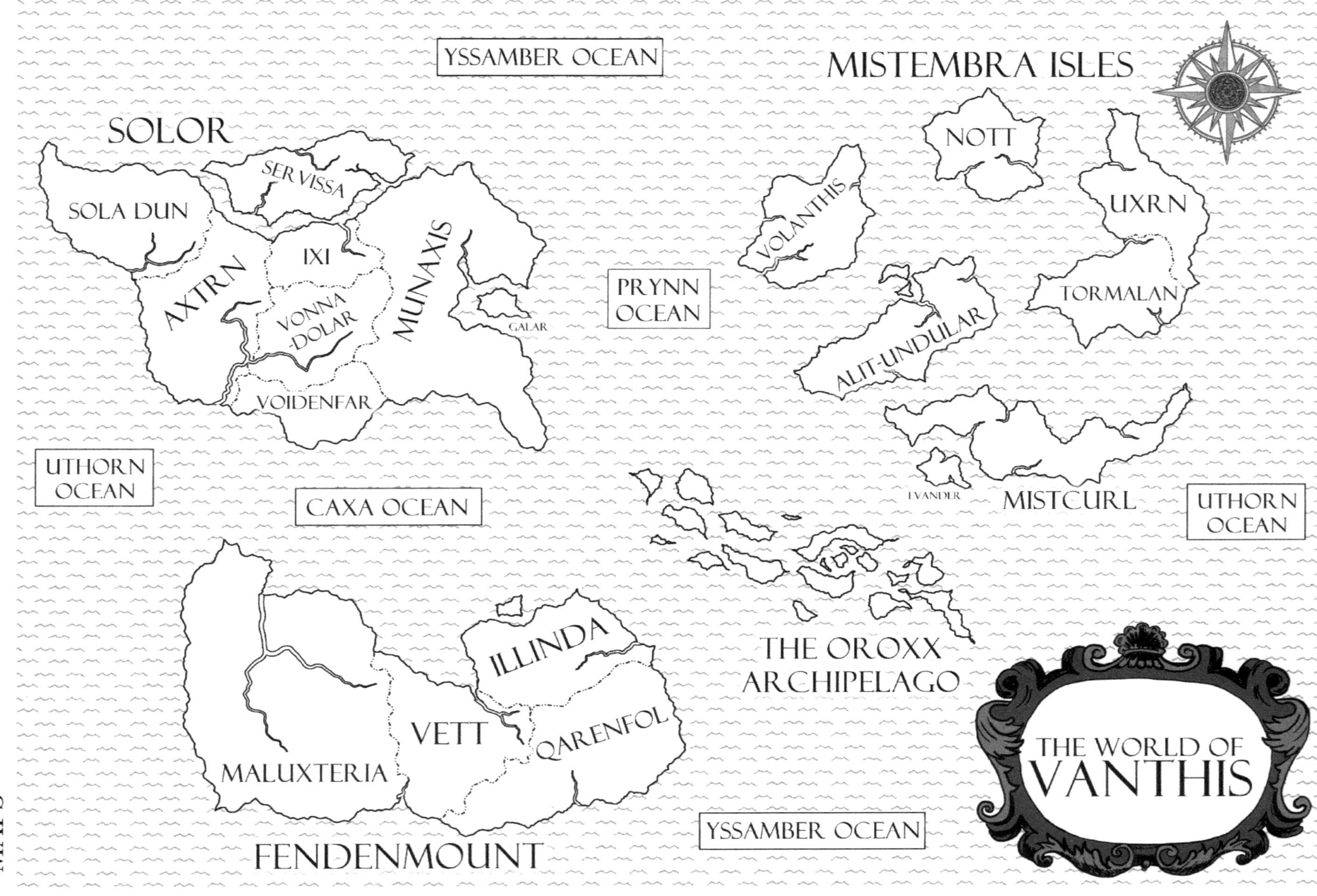
SOLOR
YSSAMBER OCEAN
MISTEMBRA ISLES
SER VISSA
SOLA DUN
AXTRN
IXI
VONNA-DOLAR
MUNAXIS
GALAR
VOIDENFAR
NOTT
VOLANTHIS
UXRN
PRYNN OCEAN
TORMALAN
ALIT-UNDULAR
UTHORN OCEAN
CAXA OCEAN
IVANDER
MISTCURL
UTHORN OCEAN
ILLINDA
THE OROXX ARCHIPELAGO
VETT
QARENFOL
MALUXTERIA
THE WORLD OF VANTHIS
YSSAMBER OCEAN
FENDENMOUNT

YSSAMBER OCEAN
NOTT
UXRN
VOLANTHIS
UTHORN OCEAN
TORMALAN
ALIT -UNDULAR
PRYNN OCEAN
EVANDER
MISTCURL
YSSAMBER OCEAN
THE MISTEMBRA ISLES

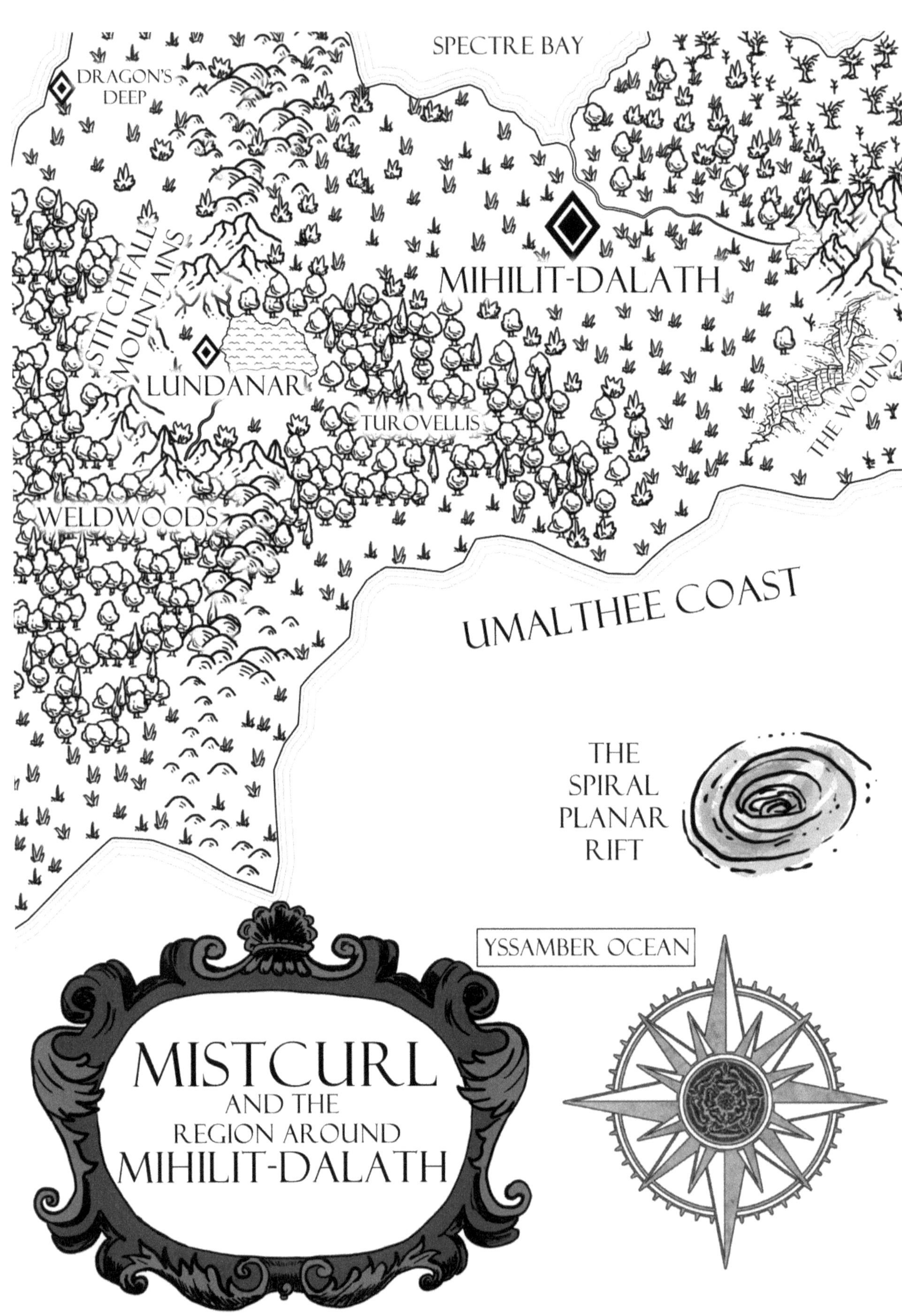

SPECTRE BAY
DRAGON'S DEEP
STITCHFALL MOUNTAINS
MIHILIT-DALATH
LUNDANAR
TUROVELLIS
THE WOUND
WELDWOODS
UMALTHEE COAST
THE SPIRAL PLANAR RIFT
YSSAMBER OCEAN
MISTCURL
AND THE
REGION AROUND
MIHILIT-DALATH

Locations of Interest

The Continents

Solor is dominated by icy mountains to the north, tundra to the southwest, and dense forests to the southeast. It is sparsely populated by many different peoples, with a large number of nomadic cultures in addition to those fixed settlements that appear. It was shaped by a grand portal to the Void in days past which dominated what became modern day Voidenfar, and many parts of the continent are shrouded in unnatural shadow or are haunted by glowing, ghostly figures at night.

Fendenmount has a hot, humid climate. Maluxteria features thick jungles, while the rest of the continent is largely dominated by dry grasslands, scrublands, and even small deserts. In days past, Maluxteria attempted to create an empire across Fendenmount, and those tensions are still felt today. Most strongly influenced by the Glamouring, especially in Maluxteria, and there is a high occurrence of fey-like wildlife.

The Oroxx Archipelago hosts a variety of cultures, with peoples varying across each island and even within the islands. Common culture includes ancestor veneration, tight family ties, and wider clans. Geographically, it is largely tropical forest and mountains. Seems generally more touched by the Astralar, with a high occurrence of crystal caves and a coast that glows eerily at night.

The Mistembra Isles have interlinked governments and cultures, and they are known for advanced magical science and arcane knowledge. Colder to the north, but temperate in Mistcurl. The focus on magical progress has lead to increasing magocracy eclipsing normal government. A number of extraplanar portals have opened up around the Isles throughout history, leading to especially magically mutated environments and wildlife.

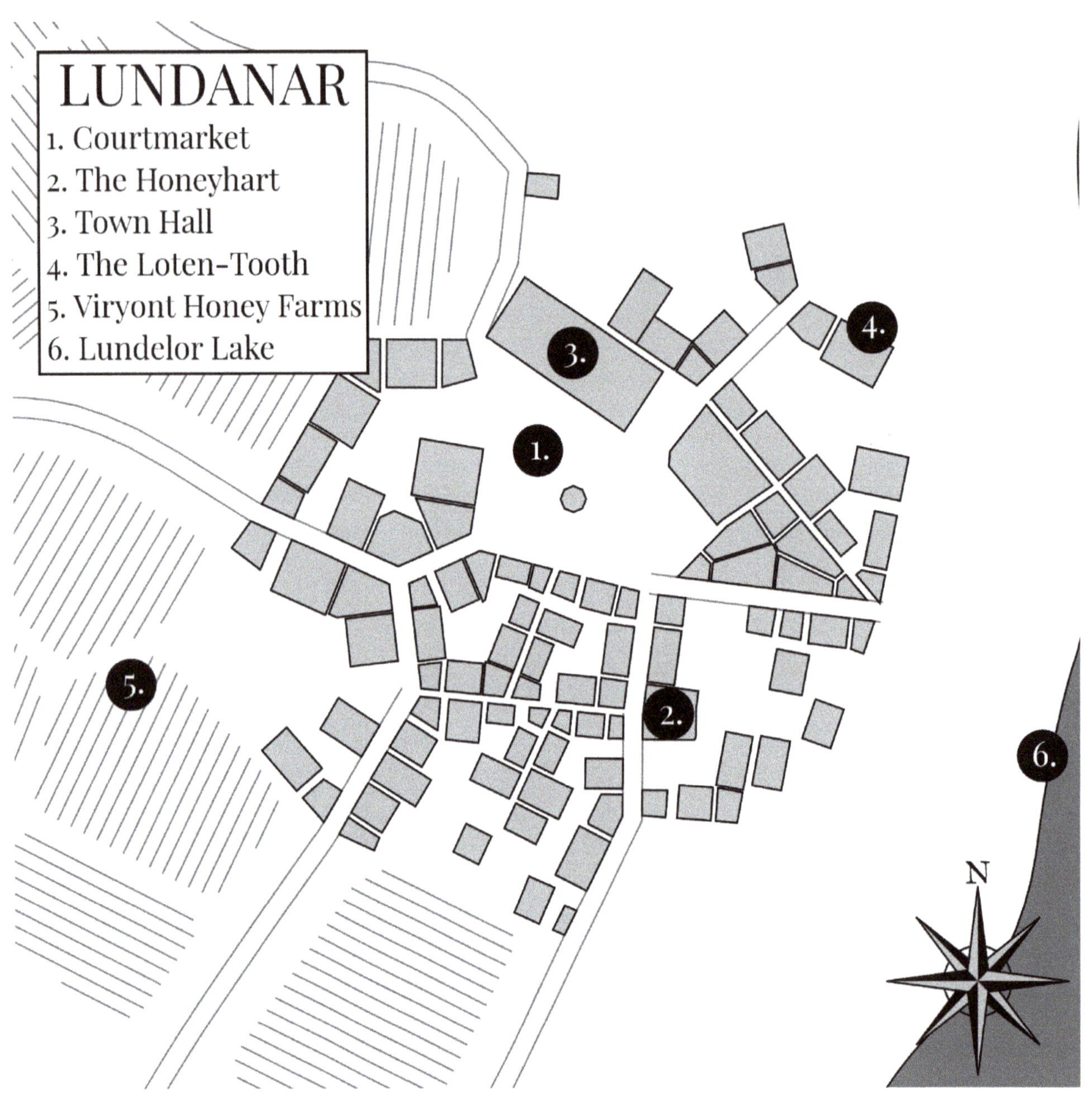

LUNDANAR
1. Courtmarket
2. The Honeyhart
3. Town Hall
4. The Loten-Tooth
5. Viryont Honey Farms
6. Lundelor Lake
1.
2.
3.
4.
5.
6.
N

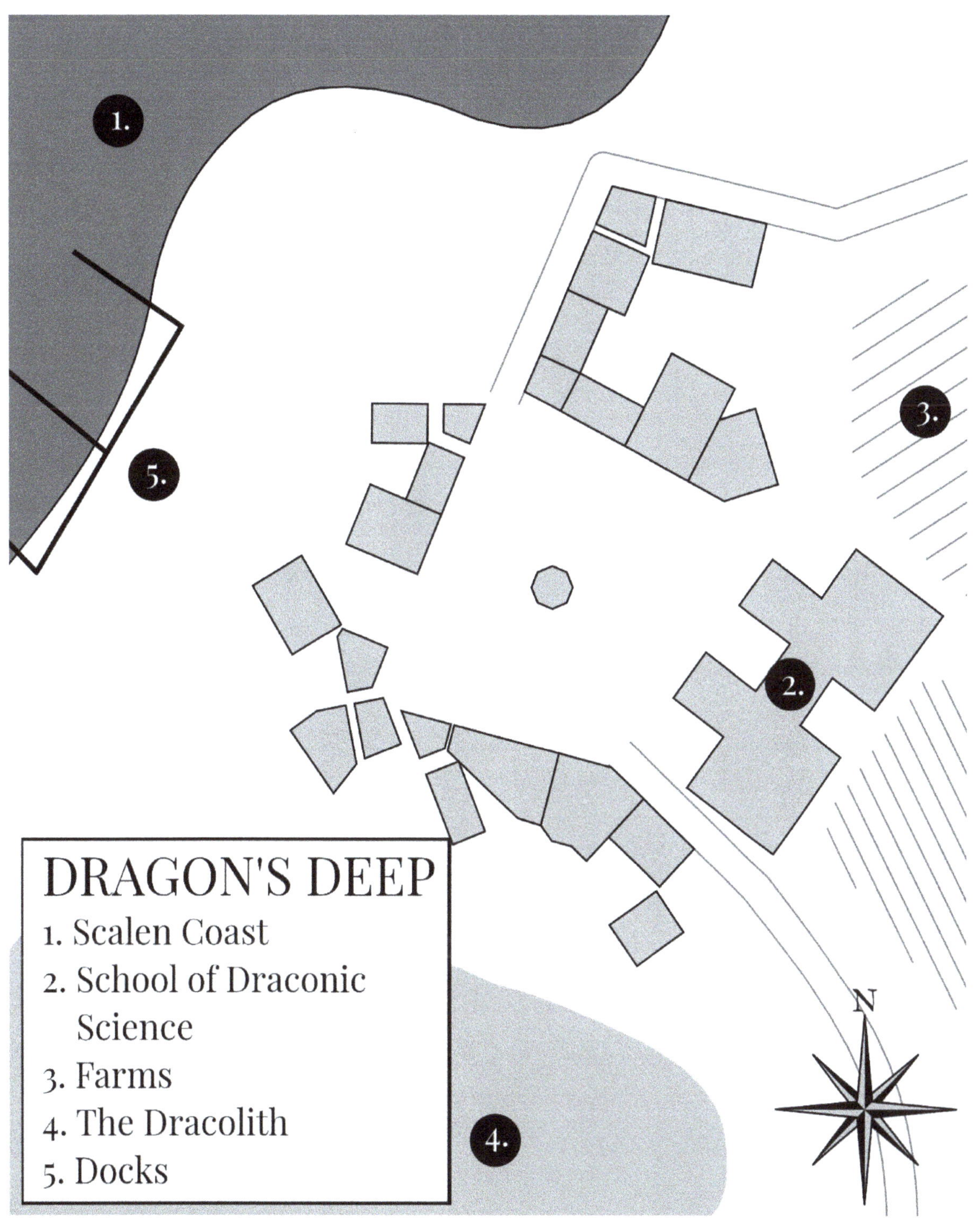

<u>Dragon's Deep, Mistcurl</u>

Dragon's Deep is a tiny coastal fishing village with an unusual history. It was settled beside an enormous, crystallised skeleton of what is believed to be a dragon. The skeleton, called The Dracolith, is nearly as large as the village itself, and is treated at times like a holy site, and at other times like an archaeological dig.

There is actually a small school in Dragon's Deep dedicated to the study of dragons and most who engage in draconic studies have spent time there. Beneath and around the village are a series of caves, some much scored as if by giant claws, giving the village its name.

MIHILIT-DALATH
1. The Verdigris Spire
2. Old Town
3. Dusk Point
4. Fenunduhn
5. Dalathi River
6. Luren Town
7. Farms
N

<u>Mihilit-dalath, Mistcurl</u>

Mihilit-dalath is the large, bustling city of Mistcurl. It is largely made of crystal, believed to have been of fey creation at one time, with crystal streets, crystal buildings, and crystal towers mixed in among the more recent buildings.

This crystal infrastructure makes it an unusually good conductor for magical energies and seems to enable it to draw from magical source. Consequently, there are powered vehicles and magically augmented buildings and lights, among other innovations, which makes it one of the most magically advanced cities in the world.

It is dominated by The Verdigris Spire, a crystal tower and citadel in which the most powerful mages of Mistcurl live and work, pooling resources and political power. It is best known as the home of the Archmage, whose power greatly eclipses that of the Mistcurl council and is considered the de facto governing force.

Also of note is Dusk Point, a ways outside the city and on the other side of the Dalathi River. It's a religious complex and monastery dedicated to Tynorilil, notable in that it was built around a garden of living crystal plants.

DEITIES AND POWERFUL ENTITIES

The world of Vanthis is full of strange and powerful entities that are worshipped, feared, or appealed to. There is some argument about the existence of some, and theologically whether deities or worship came first, but there is plenty of evidence that *some* deities and powerful entities exist, most convincingly through their use as a magical source. Generally, people are not jealous of the worship of other deities, or the lack of it. Indeed, many people are devoted to multiple deities and entities, and are certainly willing to leave offerings at the shrines and temples of other deities when passing by.

Note: There are many more deities and entities of note within Vanthis than can be listed here. This is only a taste. Game Masters and players are encouraged to create their own such entities (subject to Game Master approval).

Non-Evil Entities

Sunara, the Sun Dancer

Sunara is depicted most often as a woman with fire for hair, neatly braided into one long, flickering tail, though other details vary. She is a being of joy and celebration, with a special love of dancing. She is considered both a healer and a warrior; the cleansing flame of the sun, and the dance which crushes evil beneath her bare feet.

Mireet, the Gentle Shadow

Mireet is depicted as a hulking, shadowy beast that blots out the stars, with a vast maw of silver teeth and many limbs. Running beneath their limbs are other monstrous things: creatures of fangs and tentacles, slime and shadow. But Mireet is universally considered a benign entity. They shelter and protect those who run beneath their vast shadow form, and in all stories are shown to be slow to anger and quick to forgive. Mireet is often associated with The Void Between Worlds.

Tynorilil, the Fey Wanderer

Tynorilil is a fey being with skin like stripped bark and with crystal leaves instead of hair. Like most fey, they are a shapeshifter, though all of their forms are tree-like and with crystal leaves. They are a traveller and go wherever interests them across the planes, and are particularly beloved by gardeners and those who grow things. Tynorilil is associated with The Glamouring.

Prax, the Second Moon

There are two moons in Vanthis: Avalur and Prax. Prax is the lesser moon, and is considered an entity in their own right. They are a patron of revellers and non-violent thieves, and though they are sometimes depicted as a humanoid, the only consistency in their forms is the crescent moon upon their forehead — sometimes in a diadem, sometimes almost a tattoo.

Dragons

Dragons are beings found in all planes and all environments, and nobody is quite sure where they originated. They come in many forms: sparkling sea dragons; enormous, scaled fire dragons; sleek, feathery air dragons, and many others. But all have something almost reptilian about their countenance, and all recognise each other as fellow dragons.

They are powerfully magical, huge in size, and seem to have little interest in the affairs of humans and planarkin. Most believe they are extraplanar travellers of some kind, and some dragons are worshipped as patrons of travellers.

The Siblings

The Siblings, Ekthrentis and Orodantilla, are little-known entities: giant merpeople with tentacle hair and vast, glowing eyes. Inhabitants of the Astralar, they are associated with water, space, and stars. They are too large to travel the planes without crushing entire worlds beneath their weight, but they are gentle creatures eager to offer power in exchange for seeing new sights.

Arcanyl, The Source Personified

Arcanyl is the god of magic, known as The Source Personified. They are genderless or of shifting gender, a sparkling being of energy in the vague shape of a human. Those who study magic and draw from the arcane source often call on Arcanyl in times of need. They are said to provide knowledge to those who seek it, and to protect wizards from the dangers of Source. Arcanyl is voiceless, but is said to appear in the distance when they answer the call of their devoted.

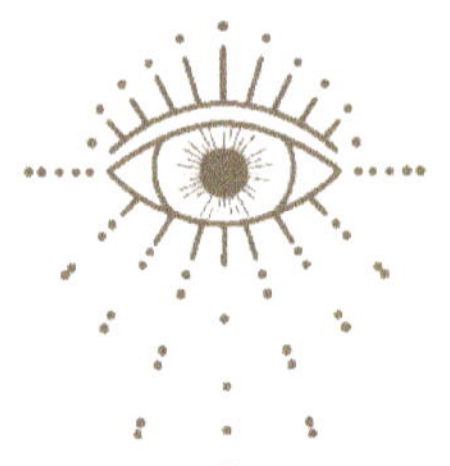

The Oracle

The Oracle is a prophesied figure from Vanthis mythology said to arise from another plane but to be made from the same stuff of Vanthis itself. The Oracle is considered omniscient, and is much favoured by scholars and those who seek knowledge. It is believed the Oracle will make a prophesy that will change Vanthis forever: a prophesied prophet. Their only identifying feature is a large, shining eye marked on their forehead. There is a cult known as the Order of the Third Eye obsessed with finding the Oracle. That cult is violent and unwelcome in most societies.

Evil Entities

Eldinithar, the Fey King

Eldinithar is a shapeshifter and cruel trickster. The only consistency in his many forms is said to be that they all wear a shining black crown. He is known for trapping people in elaborate and dangerous illusions for his own enjoyment, with a particular love for labyrinths, traps, and dungeons where nothing is what it seems. He is believed to be Fey and is known as the Fey King.

Ikkim, the Thorn Mother

Ikkim is a goddess of suffering. She has a small cult of disciples who sacrifice living creatures to a giant carnivorous plant of teeth and thorns that is Ikkim's worldly avatar. The exact location of this plant is unknown; it is possible that it can move. Her worshippers are petty, selfish people who believe that by causing suffering to others, Ikkim will reward them with wealth and power.

Loshora, the Cruel Wind

Loshora is a formless entity said to be the voice of self-hatred in people's ears. Her followers are also her victims: people who have bought into her creed of redemption through pain and rejection, people who hate themselves with religious fervour and speak cruelly to others in the hopes they will do the same. She is associated with the Void Between Worlds.

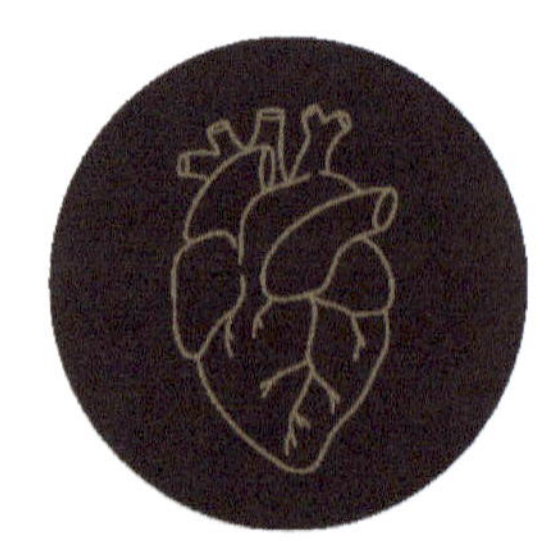

<u>Alis-Umor, the Blood Drinker</u>

Alis-Umor derives her power from violence committed in her name. She is depicted most commonly as a red shadow, and her symbol is a red chalice. Her followers are scattered and isolated. There are stories of her draining the blood from sacrificed victims, which also lends her an air of vampirism. She is associated with The Glamouring.

<u>The Knight of the Third Eye</u>

The Knight of the Third Eye is the figurehead of a cult based around finding The Oracle and manipulating their prophecy. They are referred to by many different pronouns and are depicted as wearing full plate armour etched with hundreds of eyes and their face obscured. They are said to possess magical power beyond what humans can naturally draw from a source. Their disciples are violent and also bear an eye tattoo somewhere on their body. Their ultimate aim is unknown, and they are largely ignored by governments even though they cause much trouble to the people.

ঙ NARRATIVE MODE & ACTION MODE

ꙮ NARRATIVE MODE & ACTION MODE

Narrative Mode and Action Mode delineate the less structured, story-focused part of the game from the heavily structured, mechanics-focused part of the game. Most games will have a stronger emphasis on one or the other, depending on what the Game Master and players prefer and the kind of story they are trying to tell.

NARRATIVE MODE

Narrative Mode does what it says on the tin — this mode is all about storytelling, and consequently makes up the majority of play time. Narrative Mode works by the Game Master describing a situation, its world and characters (presenting dialogue and telling the story, essentially) and then players saying what *their* characters do in response. The Game Master then describes the outcome of their actions: rinse and repeat.

The main mechanic of Narrative Mode therefore is Skill Checks. When a player presents an action, for example 'I search the room for notes', then the Game Master may request a Skill Check where the result is in some way reliant on the player character's abilities. The player makes a roll, adds it up, and declares the total. And then the Game Master describes what that total looks like — success, failure, or somewhere in-between. 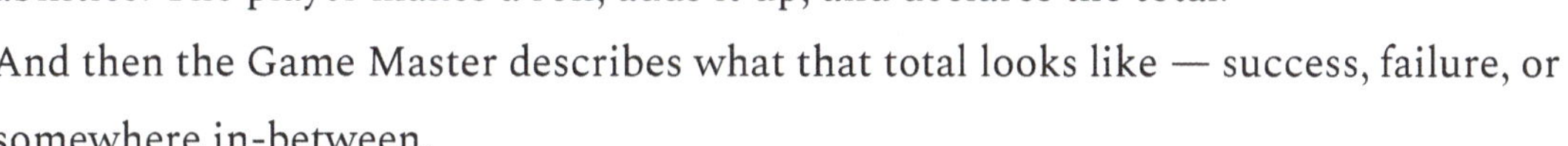

The two most important things to remember about Narrative Mode are that 1) you are telling a story and 2) it is a joint story. What this means is that Narrative Mode should never be bogged down in mechanics. It's okay not to request a Skill Check if it would interrupt the flow of the story. It's okay for a player to use a proficiency and for you not to require the specifics of that result.

 Narrative Mode is all about interaction — between the player characters and the NPCs, the player characters and the world, and the player characters and each other. The Game Master must not monopolise the storytelling time and ought to give players the chance to respond to things and take actions, but the players must be patient enough to receive the necessary information — there is no world and no NPCs, without the Game Master to describe them and play out their behaviour.

And because it is a storytelling experience, players and Game Master alike are encouraged to describe their characters' actions in detail, and to actually play out dialogue. This provides a richer experience by both painting a clearer picture and by making more for the Game Master and other players to respond to in kind. Instead of saying 'I ask the farmer what has been attacking his giant bees' and the Game Master responding 'He says it was something with big teeth', consider actually speaking out the dialogue and imbuing it with character.

This said, not all players are comfortable with this kind of interaction and safety and comfort are the most important elements of any game. It is worth talking through what the Game Master and players expect and are comfortable with in terms of role-playing before starting a game so that nobody is disappointed or made to feel uncomfortable.

GM Tip: You can handle action and combat in Narrative Mode too! Instead of having players queue for Action Mode, just continue asking for Skill Checks, Proficiencies, or even Attack Checks as part of the Narrative Mode experience. Use as much or as little of the Action Mode mechanics (eg Wound) as you choose. This is especially good for not breaking immersion and keeping up the pace! And it's ideal for encounters you want to resolve quickly.

Rest and Recovery

For ease of gameplay, healing and recovery in *Kin* do not aim for realism. You can fully heal from most Wound given a day's rest, ready to continue your adventures soon.

Rest is defined in *Kin* as a period of restful inactivity. It does not necessarily denote sleep, though the Game Master may deem sleep necessary to gain the rest effect in certain circumstances as characters *are* expected to sleep as much as a human would.

For each hour of rest, you recover the following:

Recovery per Hour		
Hours of Rest	Energy Points Recovered	Wound Healed
1	1	0
2	2	1
3	3	1
4	4	2
5	5	2
6	6	3
7	7	3
8+ (Full Rest)	Fully restored	Fully restored

ACTION MODE

Action Mode can be triggered any time the Game Master would like a more structured, turn-based approach to gameplay, and is particularly designed for handling action (eg combat, chase scenes, time-sensitive puzzles, etc). It is turn-based so players take it in turns in a set order to describe their actions.

Action Mode is always opened with queuing whereby players work out which order they will take their turns in, and is closed when the Game Master determines the action scene to have ended.

Queuing

Queuing is when players must decide between themselves in what order they will take their turn. This should be a snap judgement rather than discussion, and a note should be made of the order. Any other actors in this mode (such as NPCs controlled by the Game Master) should be added to the queue depending on both the narrative context and how efficiently the players queue.

Queuing may take place only once at the start of Action Mode, or each round, depending on the preferences of the Game Master. Queuing once can be easier to keep track of, but queuing each round gives players more flexibility.

Turn-based rounds

While in this mode, each player will get 1 turn per round, during which they will be able to take actions limited by their skills, proficiencies, and how many Action Points and Energy Points they have to spend. At the end of the round, Action Points refresh.

For example, if a player has 1 AP, they may use any proficiency or take any action that costs 1 AP (such as moving one distance class away), provided they also have the EP. Once they have used that AP, their turn is over and play moves to the next player.

Movement and Attack Range

Distance is kept to broad categories so as not to burden the Game Master with working out specific measurements, especially as Action Mode in *Kin* is all 'theatre of the mind' (eg does not use minifigures on a board).

Distance is therefore divided into 5 categories:

Movement and Attack Range		
Distance/Range	Description	Action Points (AP) to reach
Close	Within easy reach	0
Nearby	A few steps away	1
Long	A short sprint away (eg in the same room)	2
Far	Significantly beyond reach (eg another room away)	3
Distant	Visible but cannot make out the details	4 or more

In Action Mode, players will need to pay attention to distance as they will need to spend AP to move, and also because attacks have a certain Attack Range that cannot be exceeded.

<u>Attack Checks</u>

When you want to make an attack on a creature or object, you make an Attack Check. Attack Checks are similar to Skill Checks, in that you roll a Fate Die and a Weapon Die to get a result. If the total of the check is higher than the target's Defence, then the attack hits.

A basic attack does not require EP or a proficiency, and costs 1 AP.

The basic Defence of any creature is 10. This can be increased by armour, proficiencies, and other factors, but you can expect to have to hit a minimum of 10.

If you do not use a Weapon to attack, your Attack Check is Fate Die +0 to attack.

If you use a Weapon, your Attack Check is Fate Die +1 to attack.

If you roll a Fate 20 on your attack, it automatically hits. It becomes critical and deals 1 additional Wound.

If you roll a Fate 1 on your attack, it automatically misses and deals 0 Wound.

Some proficiencies increase your attack in certain circumstances, or give you Weapon Dice to add to your rolls in the place of the +1 bonus. See <u>Melee Specialist</u> and <u>Ranged Specialist</u> for more information.

Note: You cannot use ranged weapons without taking at least 1 point in the Ranged Specialist proficiency. You cannot use magic to attack without taking an appropriate Spell proficiency. You can only use simple melee weapons such as daggers, staffs, and clubs without taking at least 1 point in the Melee Specialist proficiency.

<u>Wound and Resistance</u>

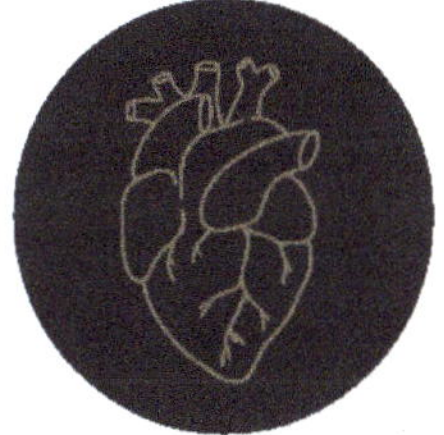

When an Attack Check meets or exceeds a target's Defence, the target receives a Wound. When a character has full Wound, they fall unconscious (or die, if that optional rule is included) until revived by healing or a full rest.

Some proficiencies increase the amount of Wound given or decrease the amount of Wound received. And some attacks have a certain kind of damage associated with them (think fire, ice, air).

Some creatures and characters have what is called Resistance to certain kinds of damage, which means they take 1 less Wound from attacks of that kind. This means, for example, that if you attack a creature that is resistant to Fire with a fireball, that creature will take 0 Wound from the attack even if it hits.

However, if the attack is critical or deals an additional Wound, then the creature will still take damage (but will take 1 less Wound than a creature that isn't resistant).

Smooth Action Mode

Smooth Action Mode is one of the two turn-based Action Modes, and focuses on speed, fluidity, and reducing interruption to the story.

Smooth Action Mode works like this:

1. Game Master presents a scenario (a chase, a ball scene, enemies attack, etc), not focusing on specifics such as how far away everything is.
2. Players queue.
3. Players take it in turns to state what action they take (eg using Proficiencies or making Attack Checks or Skill Checks).
4. Game Master looks at all the rolls presented and describes how the scene plays out, stating the actions that any NPCs took and giving out Wound as appropriate. This should resolve all the action, returning the game to Narrative Mode.

This mode focuses less on the minutiae of Action Mode and turn-based action and instead tries to reduce it to a single round and a few simple rolls, placing the emphasis on description and story.

Players should adhere to AP and EP while in this mode but there may be more flexibility, especially around movement.

Strategic Action Mode

In Strategic Action Mode, the turn-based mechanics are more strict. This mode takes longer, and will typically be more descriptive.

Strategic Action Mode works like this:

1. Game Master presents a scenario with specific details (eg who is where and how far away).
2. Players queue and the Game Master inserts any NPCs into the queue based on both the situation and how efficiently the players queue.
3. The round proceeds in a turn-based fashion, with each player character and NPC taking their turn and spending an AP and EP as they choose. Each action is described and resolved by the GM as it happens.
4. Next round, do the same again.

This mode puts the focus of a game on the mechanics and the action, and it is ideal for drawing out important encounters or for players who most enjoy action and strategy.

In this mode, there is much less flexibility around movement and mechanics as everything is carefully described across multiple rounds.

ঙ CREATE-A-CREATURE WORKSHOP

ೲ CREATE-A-CREATURE WORKSHOP

Creatures, Non-Player Characters, and other beings that players might encounter in the game may need their own stats. While for Narrative Mode purposes, players may only need to roll against a difficulty level rather than opposed to the creatures' own skill, in combat and other circumstances creatures having their own stats may be preferred (especially for those who prefer Strategic Action Mode).

Creature creation in *Kin* is kept as simple as possible. It relies on 5 main Creature Components: Maximum Wound Points, Stats, Resistances, Defence, and Special Traits & Abilities.

SAMPLE CREATURES

Creatures in Vanthis and its associated planes come in a myriad of forms, influenced often not just by one but by many planes and magical sources. Most creatures you meet will not be hostile, and even hostile creatures can be defused or avoided by a clever player.

Ferymar		
Body	Mind	Soul
5	2	3

Maximum Wound Points	Resistances	Defence	Planar Origin
◯◯	None	10	Fey

Description

Hyena-like creatures, lean and furless with a profusion of mushrooms growing along their head and spines. Their eyes are all-white and they are seemingly controlled by the fungi. Aggressive hunters that will attack even very large prey, but will flee an intimidating display of power. Non-speaking, non-sentient.

Special Traits & Abilities

Mycelial Movement: This creature can dissolve into the ground, travel by subterranean mycelial network, and re-appear and reform elsewhere. The Range for this ability is Long.

Viryont		
Body	Mind	Soul
2	5	2

Maximum Wound Points	Resistances	Defence	Planar Origin
○	None	10	Fey

Description

Viryonts are large, fluffy bees ranging in size from a bumblebee to donkey. They come in a variety of colours and some are even multiple hues. Most are domesticated but some are wild. They create honey of varying effects depending on what they are fed. Non-speaking but sentient.

Special Traits & Abilities

Swarm: this creature can summon others of its kind very quickly, even if immediately killed.

Scent Mark: harming this creature marks the one that did it, and others of its kind will attack on sight until the target is cleansed.

Sticky: this creature can stick a target in place with pollen, preventing them from moving until the pollen is removed.

Pankalar		
Body	Mind	Soul
8	3	3

Maximum Wound Points	Resistances	Defence	Planar Origin
○○○	Air / Lightning	12	Void

Description

Vampire goats. Large chimeras with the head and body of a goat, large, feathered wings tipped with claws, a lion's hind legs, a mantis' scythes for forelegs, and a long scorpion tail. They have prehensile, tube-like tongues for sucking blood and juice. They are omnivores with a preference for meat and fruit. Domesticated as mounts, they are a common form of aerial transportation, especially to and from large cities. Pankalar are generally docile. Non-speaking, non-sentient.

Special Traits & Abilities

Bloodsucker: This creature can puncture fruit and flesh with its long prehensile tongue and suck out the liquid. The Range for this ability is Nearby.
Air Bender: This creature can subtly manipulate air currents for better flight and to reduce drag on its rider. The Range for this ability is Nearby.

Mage of the Loten-Tooth

Body	Mind	Soul
2	10	8

Maximum Wound Points	Resistances	Defence	Planar Origin
○	None	10	Variable

Description

A Mage of the Loten-Tooth works for the Loten-Tooth mage tower, and it is there that they complete their studies and take on work from locals. This work commonly ranges from magical communication to magical teleportation to magical pest control. They trade in money and information, and are likely tempted by power and advancement.

Special Traits & Abilities

Mage: This character has access to magic and their attacks will likely be magical in nature.

Sealorn		
Body	Mind	Soul
2	2	2

Maximum Wound Points	Resistances		Defence	Planar Origin
○	Water / Ice		10	Astral / Fey

Description

Sealorns are chubby seal-like creatures with overlapping scales of varying colours and long, flowing fins (three to each side and one long tail). There is a large gem embedded in their chest. They have three rows of teeth and quite a nasty bite. They are most active at night and can fly — or rather, swim through the air. When travelling thus, they are suffused by a glittering astral light. Sealorn are often domesticated for their meat and eggs, but there are many in the wild.

Special Traits & Abilities

Astral Flight: This creature can swim through the air as if it was water.

CREATURE COMPONENTS

These are the main mechanical components you need to bear in mind when creating a creature to use in *Kin.*

Maximum Wound Points

You need to think about how many hits your creature can take before they die or fall unconscious. Most creatures and characters you encounter will have 1 Maximum Wound Points, though players start with 3. The aim of the game is not so much to have challenging fights as it is to problem solve and roleplay. More adventurous or combative characters may have 3-5 Maximum Wound Points.

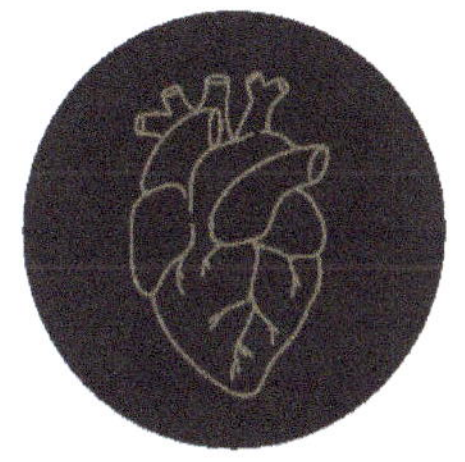

There may be particularly powerful creatures that the party is not expected to fight, or if they do, should quickly be shown to be beyond their power level. They might have as many 20 Maximum Wound Points (or even infinite, if you intend them to be unkillable by your players). No humans ought to have that many Maximum Wound Points, and any creature having more than 5 Maximum Wound Points ought to be extraordinarily rare.

When in doubt, give your creature or character 1 Maximum Wound Point.

And if you are trying to balance combat in some way, combine the Maximum Wound Points of your group. It will be an extremely challenging fight to fight a creature or creatures that combined have the same Maximum Wound Points, and they will be at risk of losing. So use the combined Maximum Wound Points or less.

Stats

Consider your creature's stats. These will primarily be used when resisting proficiencies that require Stat Checks, or when using abilities that require the target to make a Stat Check. The amount of points reflects the power and sophistication of the creature; the balance ought to reflect where it's strengths are. Is it a more cerebral or strong-willed creature, and therefore high in Mind? Is it a creature of brute muscle, and higher in strength? Is it charming or creative, and higher in Soul? Or is it an balance between two or more?

If you want a creature to be a commensurate level to certain player levels, you can check the Stat Points in the Levelling Up table and distribute them accordingly.

For ease of creation though, here are some simple pre-generated arrays of reasonably balanced Stats at various levels:

Pre-Generated Creature Stats			
Level	Low Body Array	Low Mind Array	Low Soul Array
Level 1	Body 1, Mind 2, Soul 2	Body 2, Mind 1, Soul 2	Body 2, Mind 2, Soul 1
Level 5	Body 2, Mind 4, Soul 4	Body 4, Mind 2, Soul 4	Body 4, Mind 4, Soul 2
Level 10	Body 4, Mind 6, Soul 6	Body 6, Mind 4, Soul, 6	Body 6, Mind 6, Soul 4
Level 15	Body 6, Mind 8, Soul 8	Body 8, Mind 6, Soul 8	Body 8, Mind 8, Soul 6
Level 20	Body 8, Mind 10, Soul 10	Body 10, Mind 8, Soul 10	Body 10, Mind 10, Soul 8

Defence

Defence is a measure of how difficult it is to land a hit on a creature or character. All creatures have a base Defence of 10, and this is the most common Defence total. However if a creature is armoured, especially agile, or is in some other way unusually difficult to hit, this can be slightly increased. For example, a soldier wearing casual clothes might have a Defence of 10, but in armour, might have a Defence of 11 or 12.

A human character you meet is extremely unlikely to have a Defence higher than 15, which already makes them extremely difficult to hit. Similarly, 15 is the normal maximum for any creature.

When in doubt, give your creature a Defence of 10.

Resistances

Resistances are applied to different types of damage. If a creature is resistant to a type of damage, then they take one less Wound from attacks of that type.

Most creatures and characters will not have resistances and are extremely unlikely to have more than one resistance. It's more appropriate if a creature has abilities with a specific type of damage (eg a fire elemental being resistant to fire), or if they are native to an environment where that damage is common (eg a snail that lives in a volcano being resistant to fire), but due to planar influences, some creatures or characters magically inherit a random resistance.

> When in doubt, do not give your creature a Resistance.
>
> Types of damage are: **Fire, Water / Ice, Air / Lightning, Earth**

Special Traits & Abilities

Many of the creatures and characters of *Kin* possess Special Traits or Abilities, whether those be magical or natural in nature. Some creatures might be able to teleport short distances; others might be unusually skilled acrobats or performers.

The role of the Special Traits & Abilities section is not to create an exhaustive list of everything a creature can do, but rather to highlight particular abilities of note, or remind oneself of what to expect from them.

When creating Special Traits & Abilities, it's important to bear in mind what this will mean for the party and what the limitations of these abilities are. See <u>Trait List</u> and <u>Proficiencies</u> for inspiration and examples.

Also, bear in mind that while Special Traits & Abilities are not uncommon in *Kin,* a creature or character does not necessarily need to have them, as not everyone develops their abilities to useable point.

ಖ CHARACTER SHEET

CHARACTER NAME			CHARACTER DESCRIPTION
LEVEL	UNSPENT PROFICIENCY POINTS	LUCK	

MAX WOUND POINTS	DEFENCE	ACTION POINTS	ENERGY POINTS
○○○○○			

STATS		
Body	Mind	Soul

SKILLS				
1 Point	2 Points	3 Points	4 Points	5 Points
(d4)	(d6)	(d8)	(d10)	(d12)

Body Skills		Mind Skills		Soul Skills	
Agility		Convince		Liar	
Thievery		Alchemy		Wild Empathy	
Stealth		Search		Social Instinct	
Endurance		Scholar		Perform	
Threaten		Nature		Create	

TRAITS	
Name	Description

PROFICIENCIES					
Name	Type (S, M, P)	Points	Name	Type (S, M, P)	Points

WEALTH TIER

Items Carried

Item	Amount	Item	Amount

MISCELLANEOUS

ℰℴ ACKNOWLEDGEMENTS

It is wild to think that this game is real and playable, when for the longest time it was simply a scratch document of personal notes I referenced while writing *Non-Player Character*. I've taken a lot of satisfaction from writing it; I've always wanted to create a TTRPG. How very in-character of me that the thing that finally motivated me to do it was publishing a novel based around a fictional one!

I have a few people I'd like to thank, and then I'll list the folk who need to be credited.

This was my first TTRPG and it would not be this playable (or have been published so quickly) without the help of my wonderful testers and early readers. I'd like to thank Angelica Fyfe, Kerry Paginton, and my wonderful partner Joh. I'd also like to thank Bas & Esther van Haastregt, Beni Keller, Chris Folkard, Noam Bergman, Sentinel Ark, Seth Kenlon, Sven Carpenter, and others who have chosen to go unnamed.

Thanks also to Grim for the incredible art of the characters of *Non-Player Character,* which are the gorgeous character busts and sealorns used throughout this TTRPG. It's impossible to put words to the feeling of an artist rendering your characters real and visible so perfectly. I am so grateful for your work.

I'd also like to acknowledge that this game wouldn't have existed if I hadn't played and loved so many TTRPGs over the years. While no game was a direct inspiration or mechanics source, I'd like to list the games I have read or played (and loved): Pathfinder, Wanderhome, Call of Cthulhu, MLP: RiM S3, Unknown Armies, Do: Fate of the Flying Temple, and a certain mega-popular TTRPG that prominently features lairs and lizards (I have played a good few editions of it)! Each of these has in some way shaped what I think a TTRPG looks like.

And finally, this TTRPG wouldn't have been possible without the backers of the *Non-Player Character* Kickstarter campaign. Thank you all so, so much.

ℬ CREDITS

ART

Cover art and section illustrations by Tithi Luadthong / Shutterstock.com

Character busts and sealorns by Eli Brown (Grim) (https://twitter.com/renardroi)

(Lizard person) Some artwork © 2020 Vagelio Kaliva, used with permission. All rights reserved.

White and gold dragon art by Heather Crook

Mage and cat image by MSzB / Shutterstock.com

Decorative black-and-gold line art by Kseniya Parkhimchyk / Shutterstock.com

Town and city maps created in Medieval Fantasy City Generator by Watabou

World and continent maps made in Other World Mapper

PLAYTESTERS / EARLY READERS

Angelica Fyfe	Kerry Paginton
Bas van Haastregt	Noam Bergman
Beni Keller	Sentinel Ark
Chris Folkard	Seth Kenlon
Esther van Haastregt	Sven Carpenter
Joh B	and others who have chosen to go unnamed.

ເ> ABOUT THE AUTHOR

Veo Corva writes things and reads things and reads things out loud, and sometimes they get paid for that, which is nice because it means they can feed their cat.

They live in Wiltshire with their partner and their furry familiar and as many books as they could fit in their small flat.

They are anxious and autistic and doing just fine.

To find out more about them and read more of their work, visit https://veocorva.xyz

✆ GET THE NOVEL!

Want more of this world? Read the portal fantasy novel *Non-Player Character*, out now!

Not all fantasy worlds live only in our imaginations.

32-year old Tar feels like a Non-Player Character in their own life. They've been utterly sidelined by their anxiety and they spend all their spare time playing video games. Then they get invited to play Kin, a tabletop role-playing game their friend swears will change their life. And it does, but not in the way Tar expects. Friendship, it turns out, is even better than escapism.

But what none of them knew was that it would change their life a second time. Because the world of Kin is real. And the whole party soon discovers that changing your setting doesn't change you.

Non-Player Character *is a cosy, queer portal fantasy for adults featuring a non-binary autistic protagonist and their found family of fantasy-loving nerds.*

Visit https://veocorva.xyz to find out more about *Non-Player Character* and other works by Veo Corva.